GAY AND THE PONIES

The Crown Pony Paperbacks

PONY PAGEANT
Sylvia Scott-White

A PONY TO CATCH
Elinore Havers

PONY WATCH
Elinore Havers

PONY SLEUTHS
Elinore Havers

LITTLE GREY PONY
Hilda Boden

GREY ARROW
Catherine Carey

THE GREAT PONY MYSTERY
Elinore Havers

ONLY ONE PONY
Elinore Havers

GAY AND THE PONIES
Elinore Havers

DREAM PONY
Elinore Havers

SHOW-JUMPING SUMMER
Catherine Carey

CLEAR ROUND FOR KATY
Delphine Ratcliff

In the companion hardback series

PONY GIRL
Hilda Boden

GOLDEN PONY
Delphine Ratcliff

PINK PONY
Catherine Carey

PONIES ACROSS THE RIVER
Elinore Havers

BECAUSE OF A PONY
Catherine Carey

THE NAMELESS PONY
Catherine Carey

A PONY—DOCTOR'S ORDERS
Myrtle Ellen Green

THE MERRY-MARCH PONIES
Elinore Havers

PART-EXCHANGE PONY
Myrtle Ellen Green

GAY AND THE PONIES

by

ELINORE HAVERS

LUTTERWORTH PRESS
GUILDFORD AND LONDON

First published 1964
Second impression 1971

This paperback edition first published 1976

All the animals in this story are real, the people are imaginary

The Publishers are grateful to Miss J. Kemp of Mounters Farm, Chawton, Hampshire, for permission to take the cover photograph at her riding stable

ISBN 0 7188 2254 4

PRINTED OFFSET LITHO AND BOUND IN GREAT BRITAIN
BY COX & WYMAN LTD
LONDON, FAKENHAM AND READING

CONTENTS

CHAPTER ONE

THE PUPPIES

THE puppies lay in a warm nest in their sleeping box. Frills, their mother, fed them, washed them by licking them continually and loved them. When they were a fortnight old they opened their eyes and a week later they began to walk. There were three, all were white, and the smallest one was the boldest and most active. She made little journeys across the kennel to explore when the other two had hardly started to come out of their box. She gave funny little barks, and then tumbled over from the exertion of making such a great effort.

Bridget and Robin never tired of watching them. The puppies' legs were rather wobbly at first and if they bumped into each other they fell over, but they got stronger every day, and began to play by waving a fore paw or pouncing at a brother or sister with fierce baby growls.

Their coats grew long and wavy and Frills was

kept busy licking them clean. Their father, a handsome white poodle called Fiddle-de-dee, didn't take much interest in them as yet. If asked he would have said he didn't care much for babies but preferred children who could run about and play with a ball, then he would have added hurriedly, "Not my ball, they must have one of their own." Frills thought they were wonderful.

"Aren't they sweet?" Bridget said, for about the hundredth time.

"Super!" Robin agreed. "Look at that one sitting down to practise barking, a silly little squeaky bark but he's doing his best!"

"It's time they began to learn to lap," said Mrs. Denley, the children's mother. "We'll start teaching them today."

They took a saucer full of warm baby-food out to the kennel and Frills jumped up, hoping it was for her.

Robin said, "It's not for you, Frilly, but perhaps there'll be some over you can have."

"May I have this one to teach?" Bridget asked, picking up the smallest. "It's my favourite."

"Yes, but don't delay because the food mustn't get cold. Dip your finger in and let it lick some off it. Now put its nose in the saucer."

"It's beginning to lap," cried Bridget. "Oh dear! It's put a paw in the saucer."

In no time all the puppies could lap. A good deal of milky food was spread over their funny little faces and several paws had been dipped in too, but Frills licked them clean without having to be asked.

Then the puppies had a scamper round their pen before going to lie in a warm heap on top of each other in their box. Later Mrs. Denley clipped their faces to make it easier to keep them clean. "They look like little hedgehogs!" she said. "And they wriggled terribly but I don't think they really minded the clippers."

"It'll be fun when they're old enough to come out on the lawn to play," said Robin.

"I like the little one best," Bridget said.

"Don't forget we aren't keeping any of them for good," her mother said. "Frills and Fiddle are quite enough. The puppies will have to be sold."

"Frills will be sad," said Bridget.

"Yes, poodles love their puppies for a long time," Mrs. Denley said; "most animals forget them fairly soon but not poodles. But we'll find the puppies good homes."

In another fortnight the puppies came out on

the lawn for a little while each fine day. Bridget and Robin lay on the grass and watched them.

"The darling little one!" Bridget said. "She's the sweetest and the bravest, I wish we could keep her."

By now they were having four meals a day, two of baby-food and two of minced meat with brown bread crumbs, and they grew fast, but Bridget's favourite remained the smallest. She was the gayest and the naughtiest. She knew Mrs. Denley and Bridget and Robin. They brought her food and picked her up and cuddled her. She liked them. She knew the lawn and the flower beds near it. There were nice things there which the puppies pulled and ran about with in their mouths.

"They look very pretty carrying flowers," said Mrs. Denley, "but it's not at all good for the flower beds! They seem to choose purple and blue ones, those must be colours they see clearly."

"We'd better plant a special assortment of pansies for the poodles to pick," Mr. Denley said, "they're not leaving many of these for us!"

When the puppies went anywhere new, on to the drive, or round to the garage or into the vegetable garden, they looked round anxiously and put their tails down, then they would scamper back to the lawn or to their kennel where they felt safe because they knew it.

Frills played with them, rolling them over and pretending to growl, and she liked sitting in the sun watching them, her lovely dark eyes shining with pride and love for them.

She gave them good advice. "You must do what humans want, no matter how silly it seems. It saves a lot of unpleasantness if you fall in with their wishes over such things as not putting muddy paws on their clothes or going outside if you feel sick. Humans are very fussy." She rolled the smallest puppy over and licked it. "I hope you will all get a nice master and missus," she went on, "ones with motor cars; we poodles enjoy motoring and they ought always to keep a car for us, and remember that the best place to sleep is on Missus' bed. It's sure to be the most comfortable place and if you're not allowed there try for the best sofa. They may push you down but keep getting up again and they'll probably give in before you do."

The largest puppy stopped chewing one of his sisters' ears to say, "I mean to get my own way wherever I go to live."

"Quite right!" said Frills. "Poodles' feelings must be considered, we aren't like ordinary dogs;

but remember, puppies, we are much more intelligent than ordinary dogs and humans expect us to be clever. I hope you will live up to our reputation."

"I hope I go to a nice Missus," said the little puppy.

"So do I, my dear," Frills said. "A dog's Master or Missus is the most wonderful person in the world to him, but some of them are rather thoughtless about us sometimes. But you must always look after them. Humans can't do without us to look after them and their property. Wonderful though they are, they have to rely on us to know when there's a burglar about, or a strange cat in the garden, or even a piece of something gone bad. They haven't got proper noses, you see."

"I hope my Missus won't want me to learn tricks," said the other puppy, "because I won't. So there!"

"If you ever have any trouble with your Missus," said Frills, "you can make her look silly by refusing to come when she calls you, just keep out of reach and politely wag your tail. You may get a scolding when she does catch you, but it's worth it"—Frills sniggered—"she'll look so silly, but don't do it often."

The puppies listened attentively and remembered everything she said.

That afternoon Bridget and Robin took the puppies on to the lawn to let them play.

"They're rather like the Three Bears!" Bridget said. "One's big and one's little and the other one comes in the middle."

"The big one's a fine chap!" Robin said, rolling him over and tickling him, while the puppy tried to eat Robin's finger. "It's going to thunder, we'll have to put them in again. Look at those inky black clouds. I heard thunder in the distance."

The sun went in and the sky became dark. Mrs. Denley called from the house, "Robin! Will you run to the pillar box with these letters for me? Hurry, it's going to rain."

Robin took the letters and ran off. Bridget thought she'd put her bicycle away. It was a new one and she didn't want it to get wet. Should she leave the puppies? They couldn't come to any harm.

"Look after them, Frills," she said. "I won't be a minute." And she took her bicycle round to the back of the house to the bicycle shed.

As she came out of the shed there was a loud

clap of thunder. The next minute the rain came pelting down.

"Oh, the puppies!" thought Bridget. "They'll be frightened of the thunder. And they'll get wet."

She rushed round the house, but when she reached the lawn neither Frills nor the puppies were to be seen.

Where could they be? Bridget ran into the porch out of the rain and looked across the garden. Not a sign of them.

Robin came running up the drive. "Didn't quite make it!" he panted. "I thought I'd get in before the storm. Did you hear that loud crash? Wasn't it a snorter!" His hair was plastered down and his shirt had wet patches on the shoulders.

"I can't find the puppies," Bridget said. "I went to put my bike away and the thunder started. I tore back but they'd gone. And Frills too."

"Gosh! Are they out in this?" said Robin. "Awfully bad for them to get wet, I should think."

"And they'll be frightened," said Bridget anxiously. "Oh——" There was another loud clap of thunder. "Poor little things! Where can they be?"

"Perhaps Frills has taken them back to the

kennel," suggested Robin. "I'm going to put my mack on and look."

"So will I," said Bridget bravely, for she didn't like thunder. "Why, here's Frills. But where are the puppies? What have you done with them, Frilly?"

"I can hear them," exclaimed Robin. "Upstairs."

They ran up and found two puppies on the landing, whimpering and looking down the stairs at Frills.

"They don't know how to come down," said Robin. "They haven't been upstairs before. I bet I know what happened. Frills always hides under a bed in a thunderstorm, and she tried to take the puppies too."

"And all the bedroom doors are shut," said Bridget. "So she couldn't. But the little one isn't here. What can have happened to it? I hope it isn't outside in the rain."

Frills ran downstairs and went into the sitting-room. The children, each carrying a puppy, followed her. She went across to Mrs. Denley's writing desk and sniffed under it. She snorted and wagged her tail. Robin knelt down and looked.

"The puppy! It's a tight squeeze. I can't think

how it got in and I daren't try and pull it out, it might hurt it. It's almost wedged."

"It crawled under when there was that loud thunder, I expect," Bridget said. "But how can we get it out?"

Robin sat back on his heels. "It's an awfully tight fit but it got in so it can come out. Let's go away and see if it comes out on its own."

They went out of the room and waited, peeping in at the door to see what happened. Very soon a little head appeared and the puppy squeezed itself out and galloped across the room to them.

"Clever pup!" said Bridget, lifting her up. "This is the one who does things that are different. Perhaps she's going to have adventures."

It wasn't long before the puppies were old enough to go to their new homes. Some people came and bought the largest one, leaving the two little sisters.

"I wish we could keep the little one," Bridget said. "Couldn't we, Daddy?"

"I think not, two dogs are enough," he replied.

"Perhaps nobody will buy her," Bridget said hopefully.

When two ladies came to see the puppies Bridget watched anxiously as they looked first at one puppy and then at the other and tried to make up their minds which one to have.

"This little one is very sweet, she has such a pretty little face."

"But the larger one may be sturdier, and perhaps bolder," said the other lady.

"The little one hid when there was a thunderstorm," Bridget told them. "I should have the larger one."

They looked at them both again and Bridget held her breath until one of them said, "I think we'll have the bigger one."

After they'd gone Bridget cuddled the puppy, who licked her chin and snuggled up to her neck. "We've still got my favourite."

"You mustn't try to put people off that one," said her mother, "because we don't want to keep another dog."

"But she's so sweet. Couldn't she be mine?"

"No. She must go when we find her a nice home. But we can't leave the poor little thing in the kennel alone so she'll have to come and live indoors. But don't get too fond of her, darling."

"There's nothing easier than getting fond of a poodle puppy," Bridget said as the puppy bit her ear and nibbled her fingers. She helped to train the puppy to sit in her basket, to wear a collar and to walk on a lead. They called her Gay because she was so full of play, and, as nobody seemed to want a puppy just then, she stayed with the Denleys. She went everywhere with them and Frills and Fiddle, and they all loved going out in the car. A special treat for them, and for Bridget and Robin, was to go for a picnic on the downs where Robin and Fiddle would run while Frills and Gay romped with Bridget. But when Gay was about six months old a big change came into all their lives.

CHAPTER TWO

A NEW HOME FOR GAY

THE poodles became aware that something unusual was about to take place in the Denley family. There were lots of discussions, cupboards were turned out, the children were very excited and the poodles could sense the excitement.

"What's going on? Robin hasn't played with my ball and me for days," complained Fiddle.

"It's either spring cleaning or going away for the summer holidays, only it's worse than usual," said Frills. "I sat on the sofa this morning and nobody told me to get down."

"And they left the kitchen cupboard door open," Gay said.

"Have you been at the sugar?" Fiddle asked sternly.

"Poodles never steal," said Frills, very righteously.

Gay remembered Frills helping herself to a chocolate biscuit off the lower shelf of the tea trolley when it had been left standing in the hall, but Frills thought food put at a dog's nose level was for dogs.

"I wonder why they're so excited," Gay said.

"It's like when they're going to church on Sunday morning and leaving us at home," said Frills. "Only more important than a Sunday, and it's not Christmas because it hasn't the right smell."

"What does Christmas smell of?" asked Gay.

"Turkey cooking!" said Fiddle gloatingly. "Chocolate and toffee in stockings in bed in the morning!"

"Whatever for?" interrupted Gay.

"The children have them and we help open them," said Frills. "We taste things, it's the only time they let us have sweets. Mrs. Denley says they aren't good for dogs."

"And people come shouting at the door in the dark and we have a lot of barking to do," Fiddle told Gay.

"They shout a lot and get oranges and money given them," said Frills. "They like the shouting; they stop us barking—which sounds much nicer, I think—to listen to the shouting."

"I shall like Christmas," said Gay.

But they were not going to spend Christmas together, for the poodles learned that the Denleys were going across the sea to live in somewhere called New Zealand. Bridget and Robin were very excited and were longing to start on the sea voyage. The poodles discovered that Fiddle and Frills were going too, but Gay was to be left in England.

Bridget had pleaded for her to go too, but Mr. Denley said, "No. We never intended keeping her, and as it is very expensive to take dogs, two is all we can take. Gay isn't too old to settle happily in a new home."

"I'm sorry to leave her," said Mrs. Denley, "but two will be quite enough to look after and when we get out there Frills can have some more puppies. We will choose a really happy home for Gay."

Inquiries were made and several people wanting a poodle came to see Mrs. Denley. The first was a lady who lived in a flat. Mrs. Denley said as Gay was used to living in the country with a garden to play in she didn't think she'd be happy in a flat. The next lady went out to work and proposed leaving Gay shut up alone all day. Mrs. Denley turned her down too. The third lady lived in the country and had a garden. She had a little girl called Barbara who was the same age as Bridget, and who longed to have a poodle, so Mrs. Denley said she would give them Gay.

One of the last drives in the car before leaving for New Zealand was to take Gay to her new home. Bridget shed some tears, and Robin and Mrs. Denley had lumps in their throats when they parted with her.

Gay stood shivering with nervousness when the Denleys drove away. Her new owner, Barbara Mason, held her lead and said, "It's marvellous. I've always wanted a poodle."

Mrs. Mason was a lady who was always busy, and she was slap-dash and forgetful, always in a hurry, and grumbling about how much she had to do. Mrs. Denley had thought she seemed kind but she was inconsiderate. Barbara was spoilt and selfish. She made a great fuss of Gay at first. She took her out on a lead to show to all her friends and she brushed her every day for several days. She gave her lots of tit-bits.

Mrs. Denley had fed the dogs twice a day at regular times and had not allowed tit-bits between meals. On being given chocolates and ice cream at all times of the day Gay lost her appetite. Her meals were given her at irregular times; soft and sloppy with nothing to crunch, her teeth became dirty and she had indigestion. Barbara often forgot to rinse and refill her water bowl, sometimes it was empty for several days and Gay went thirsty.

Barbara thought she'd teach Gay some tricks. She took her out in the garden and tried to make her jump through a hoop. Gay had no idea what she was expected to do. Barbara became impatient; putting Gay on a lead she tried to drag her through the hoop. Gay was frightened and resisted, digging her nails into the ground.

"Silly little thing," Barbara said crossly. She gave her a biscuit and tried to lead her through the hoop but Gay was frightened now and crouched down, refusing to move.

Barbara gave up and Gay ran indoors and hid under the stairs, where she stayed until the house was quiet. Barbara went out to tea and did not return until supper time when she talked about a new game they'd played.

"Have you given Gay her supper?" asked Mrs. Mason.

"Oh bother! Can't you, Mummie?"

"She's your dog, Barbara. You promised to look after her."

"She's silly. Need I go to bed at once? Then I can show you the game."

Mrs. Mason agreed, and Barbara stayed up playing the card game and forgot Gay's supper.

Gay became thin and nervous. She was lonely, missing Frills and Fiddle and all the fun she'd had with Bridget and Robin, and, most of all, the affection which the Denleys had had for their dogs. Her coat was neglected and her toe nails became too long for she didn't get enough exercise to wear them down and was never taken to have them trimmed.

"That dog needs clipping," Mrs. Mason said one day. "Her coat's grown very untidy. I'll ring up for an appointment tomorrow."

"Oh not tomorrow, Mummie," Barbara exclaimed. "You said we could go for a picnic. Jennifer and Richard are coming to tea."

"So they are. A picnic would be nice. We'll go up on the downs and you can exercise Gay. We must get a new disc for her collar with your name on it. I took the one with the Denleys' name off."

As Gay lay in her basket that night the moon shone in through the window, making a bright patch on the floor. Gay wished she was back with the Denleys, with Frills and Fiddle in their baskets.

The bright moonlight made her feel so miserable that she began to howl. Mrs. Mason came downstairs in her dressing-gown. She was very cross. She told Gay to be quiet and smacked her.

Gay lay cowering in her basket with her heart beating fast, harsh voices and crossness frightened her. Mrs. Denley had never smacked her, for she thought poodles so sensitive that scolding was usually sufficient punishment.

It hadn't occurred to Mrs. Mason to draw the curtain to shut out the moonlight and it shone on Gay, making her want to bark and howl. But she didn't dare.

Next morning Mrs. Mason was still cross from having had her sleep disturbed and Gay kept out of her way until it was time to start for the picnic.

"You are lucky having a poodle," said Jennifer, when they got into the car to drive to the downs.

"She's my own," said Barbara, who loved showing off her dog to her friends.

"Can she do any tricks?" asked Richard.

"No. But I'm going to teach her some."

Gay's heart sank at hearing this. When they reached the downs Gay sniffed. "I've been here before," she thought. Memories of Robin and Bridget, Frills and Fiddle crowded into her head, exciting her. Somewhere here she'd played with Frills; Robin and Fiddle had run over the grass, and they'd all been together, happy in the sunshine. She thought perhaps if she ran over the green hills which stretched away on all sides, she'd find Frills and Fiddle and they'd all be together again.

At that moment Barbara took off her lead. Gay hesitated for a minute and then ran away. When she had gone a little way she heard Barbara and Mrs. Mason calling, but she went on across the downs.

Soon she was out of sight of the Masons. She kept on, hoping to smell something which would lead her to Bridget and Frills but there were no familiar scents.

Presently she stopped and looked round. Nothing but grass in every direction. She was lost.

CHAPTER THREE

GAY IS A PRISONER

GAY had run fast for quite a long way and she was beginning to feel tired. She stood still and sniffed into the wind, but no familiar scents came to her clever, sensitive little nose. Her tail drooped, she was anxious and lonely as she gazed over the deserted downs. Somewhere, she thought, were Frills and Fiddle, and the kind Denleys—if only she could find them.

She went on slowly, stopping now and again to look round, to sniff, and to whine anxiously. Presently she came to a cart track; it smelt of humans, strange ones, but she followed it hopefully. It led downhill and soon she reached a small village.

It was dark and getting cold as she went past the cottages where lights were appearing in the windows. Inside people were having supper, dogs and cats were lying on cosy cushions or warming themselves by a fire, but poor little Gay stood in the road, looking about her and shivering, feeling very miserable.

A man came by and turned towards the gate of one of the cottages. Then he saw Gay.

"Hello! Where do ye come from? Not hereabouts, I know." He went towards her. "Come on then. Come 'ere."

Gay retreated a little and he stooped down, snapping his fingers and calling to her, but she kept out of reach.

He stood and looked at her. "Valuable," he muttered, "that's what that dog is, and no one else is a-going to 'ave it." He went in at the gate and entered the cottage. Gay watched. She didn't like the man, she had an uneasy feeling about him, but she wanted company. Very soon the man came back, hurrying; it was dark and he didn't see Gay at once for she had gone a little way up the lane towards the downs. Her wise instinct told her to escape but because she was young and unused to looking after herself she lingered, hoping the man would be a friend to her.

"Where's that dawg got to?" the man grumbled. "It's worth a tidy sum, I reckon. Lost, I dessay, and there'll be a reward." Then he saw her, white against the darkness and with her eyes shining.

"Come on, then," he coaxed, stooping down and holding out his hand. "Come on, little 'un."

Gay sniffed. Meat! She was hungry and it was very tempting. She came a little nearer. Something told her to go back, to run away, but the smell of the meat was too much for her. She crept forward and stretched out to take some. A rough hand grabbed her. "Got yer." Gay struggled but he held her firmly and carried her into his cottage. She was shivering with fright as the man kicked the door to and examined her collar. "No name nor address," he said. "Shame, that's what it is. I could 'a got a reward for taking it 'ome. Still, I can sell it."

He put Gay in a shed at the back of the cottage. There was a packing case with some straw in it, and he turned it on its side so she could get in to sleep there. Gay stood looking unhappy and dejected in the dim light of his lantern. He fetched her a few scraps of bread and gristly meat in a broken saucer and a bowl of water. Then he left her.

Gay sniffed at the food and drank some water. She was too scared and miserable to want to eat. Then she went round the shed, sniffing at everything and looking for a way out. The door was strong and fitted without any cracks or gaps where a little dog could try to squeeze and the walls were of thick planks. It was a prison. She slept little that night, the straw in the wooden case was not good clean bedding straw but musty damp straw that had been used for packing, and apart from discomfort she was too unhappy to sleep. She thought of Frills and Fiddle and wished she could find them. She couldn't know they were in a ship steaming towards New Zealand with all the Denleys.

In the morning the man seemed upset to find she hadn't eaten her supper. He brought her some bread and milk, she lapped a little, and then he went away leaving her shut in the shed.

Gay listened to his footsteps going down the path, the gate opened and then shut with a click, the man got on his bicycle and rode away to work.

Everything was quiet. Gay wandered round the shed which was cluttered up with firewood, gardening tools, a wheelbarrow and a hen coop. She drank the rest of the milk and wandered round again restlessly. She had only one thought—to get away.

She scratched in a corner of the shed. The floor was of hard earth but it was loose in a corner where a rat had made a hole. It was soft to her paws and she began to dig.

She worked all day. Several times she heard someone pass in the lane and she stopped and listened anxiously. She rested for a short while two or three times, but she was so eager to escape that she kept on digging most of the day. Occasionally she came up against a big stone and tried to pull it out with her teeth; her forepaws became quite tender and she wore her nails down short but still she kept on digging. The hole became quite large and she was tunnelling under the shed by evening. The soft soil had only been on the top and she had found it very hard and stony, but the hope of escaping kept her going. Digging furiously with her forepaws and scraping the loose earth away with her hind legs, Gay kept at her task.

At dusk she heard the gate click and she stopped digging to listen. The man was coming up the path. Gay darted into her tunnel and scraped at the earth with new energy. She knew she was nearly at the surface outside the shed. Driving upwards her paws met soft soil, a few vigorous strokes and her muzzle came out into the fresh air. She struggled up and broke out. She shook herself and trotted down the garden path. She was free!

Then the door of the cottage opened and a shaft of light streamed over the path. Gay ran towards the gate but it was too late. The man had seen her and with a shout he started in pursuit. Gay fled, her heart thumping with fear.

The gate was shut. Panic-stricken, she ran along the fence looking for somewhere she could get through, or squeeze under—anywhere that she could wriggle out.

The man's footsteps pounded behind her, closer and closer. Gay was in a strange place where she didn't know her way about and she could only run on, in the dark, hoping to find a way out. She ran beside the hedge until she found herelf cornered beside a hen house. She turned and tried to dodge back but the man was too close to her. He caught her. Grasping her by the scruff of her neck he swung her up under his arm and went back to the cottage.

First he fetched a lantern. Then he went to the shed for he couldn't think how she had got out. He was feeling cross, having stopped on his way home to make inquiries as to whether anyone had lost a poodle and was offering a reward, but he could not hear of any such thing. As soon as he flashed the light round inside the shed he saw the heap of loose earth and then the tunnel which Gay had worked so hard to make.

"Dig yer way out, would yer?" he said crossly. Putting her down on the ground he beat her. Gay cried and lay shivering and whimpering. She had never been harshly treated and she was terrified. It was a great shock to her to find a human could be unkind, for she had never met cruelty before, and she trusted them.

The man took her into the cottage and put her in the back kitchen. He threw down a sack for her to lie on and gave her a plate of scraps. Gay was too frightened to eat. She lay on the sack all night, whimpering a little and quivering; she was bruised and sore.

In the morning the man came in to see her. He was annoyed to find she hadn't eaten anything. If she became ill he wouldn't be able to sell her. He tried to coax her to eat but Gay backed away and wouldn't let him come near her.

The man grumbled. "Got to get 'er to eat summat. Wonder if she'd take an egg?" He unlocked the back door and went out, shutting it behind him quickly so that Gay shouldn't escape.

She sat watching the door. That was the way to freedom. In a few minutes he came back carrying several eggs; he slipped in quickly and shut the door but he didn't lock it.

He broke an egg into a dish and began to stir it with some milk he had added. Heavy steps sounded outside. There was a knock on the door and then it was thrown open. A big, red-faced man looked in saying, "Morning, George. Can you lend me——"

"Look out! Shut the door," shouted George.

Too late. Gay had seen a chance and had taken it. Nerving herself to approach the strange man she slipped past him and ran down the path. In daylight she could see all round and she meant to escape this time.

Then her heart bounded. The gate had been left open! Gay turned up the lane to the downs without thinking, because it was the way she'd come and was familiar. If she had gone the other way into the village she might have been caught but in the open she could run away.

The two men ran after her calling and shouting but she soon left them behind and found herself on the bare, lonely downs again.

She went slowly, not knowing which way to turn, and feeling tired. She had had very little food or sleep for two days and nights and the work on the tunnel had tired her.

She kept on, stopping sometimes to look round and to sniff, and then going on again, more and more slowly. Once she lay down to rest but loneliness and hunger drove her on.

When she came to a track she followed it, limping a little for she was footsore; she made her way down the cart track from the downs to a valley where there were fields, woods and a river. She crossed a field and the track turned in to a farm.

Gay hesitated. She wanted to find people, someone to take her in and feed her and care for her. But the man at the cottage had shaken her faith in humans and she was afraid. If she had only known, there was a girl at the farm who loved dogs and who would have given her all she wanted, but as she hesitated she heard a man's voice, it scared her and she limped on. On across the endless green fields. Where would she find food and shelter?

As Gay was nearing the river which flowed through the fields she heard barking. Looking back she saw a big farm dog. She trotted on faster. She was not used to going about alone and she had not met many big dogs; made nervous by all that had happened to her, she ran away.

The big dog would not have hurt her but when she began to run he immediately chased her.

Tired and footsore, Gay felt desperate; though she ran her fastest the big dog was gaining on her. She was too frightened to know what she was doing and she dashed into the river. The cold water made her gasp but she swam bravely. The river was wide, for it overflowed its bank just there, and a line of willows standing in the water marked its true course.

It cost Gay a great effort to swim out to the trees, and when she reached them and found a fallen tree trunk she had to put all her remaining strength into dragging herself out of the water.

The big dog stopped at the water's edge, barked once or twice, and then trotted back to the farm.

Gay crouched on the fallen tree trunk, wet and cold, without the energy to go any farther.

CHAPTER FOUR

RESCUED BY A PONY

THAT autumn afternoon Penny and Joanna Maitland were out riding on their ponies, Kim and Twinkle.

"Now school's started we shan't get much riding," said Penny.

"And the evenings will start to get dark early soon," said Joanna, "we'll have hardly any time out of doors."

"Bother school!" Penny said. "Kim's going nicely now and jumping well, it's a pity to have to stop riding regularly. And he gets bored when he isn't ridden and he breaks out of his field."

"Twink doesn't follow him, luckily," Joanna said.

"The trouble is, Kim's too clever!" said Penny. "He can open gates or jump or squeeze or wriggle out of any field."

Kim was a dark brown with a long black mane and tail and the fawn mealy nose of an Exmoor pony. Twinkle was a little dark brown Dartmoor pony, with a very long tail and a smartly hogged mane. He had a perky, cheeky little head.

Penny opened the gate into a field and held it for Joanna and Twinkle; she made Kim go up to the gate while she latched it.

"Now for a canter!" said Joanna and set Twinkle going.

Kim wheeled round and galloped after them. Penny steadied him and as soon as he had his head in front he settled down. He had a long, comfortable stride, and Twinkle, a smaller pony, had all he could do to keep up.

At the far end of the field they pulled up and Joanna said, "Twink and I can never beat you and Kim!"

They came out into a lane and Joanna asked, "Which way shall we go home? The long way round or by the river?"

"The long way's nice, as we can get a good canter across the big meadow."

"But if we go by the river we might see a kingfisher," Joanna said. "Do let's."

"All right," agreed Penny.

They trotted down the lane and into the field, where a short ride along the river would bring them out on the road towards their home.

Joanna was watching the river. Penny was thinking about her pony; she was stroking his mane down. One bit always fell over on the wrong side and she wondered how she could train it to lie down properly.

"No kingfisher," said Joanna. "Shall we wait a minute? We might see one."

"No, come on. It'll be tea-time."

"Oh, just a minute," pleaded Joanna. "I'd love to see one."

Several minutes passed and Penny said, "Come on, Jo."

They rode on, Joanna looking back and hoping to see the glorious flash of blue-green.

"Penny," she called. "Wait a minute."

"Why? Do come on, Joanna." Penny rode on.

"No, wait. There's something there—Penny, look!" Joanna had pulled up and was pointing. "Look, on that fallen tree. It's a white animal, a cat? No, it's——"

"It's a dog. I think it's drowned."

"Oh no!" cried Joanna. "How awful."

"We'll soon see."

Penny turned Kim and cantered back; reaching the water's edge she pulled up. The distance was short and she could see plainly.

"I believe it's a poodle. However did it get there?"

"Is it dead?" asked Joanna. She was nearly in tears.

"It's lying very still," Penny said anxiously. "Hi, poodle! Good dog!" she called.

Gay was lying on the tree trunk, exhausted and cold. She heard voices, children's voices which reminded her of Bridget. She raised her head and looked round.

"He moved!" shouted Joanna. "Oh, how can we get him?"

"I'll get him. You stay here," ordered Penny. "I'll get him somehow," she said through her clenched teeth and rode Kim into the water.

Kim went in slowly and reluctantly.

"Is it deep?" called Joanna. "Will you be able to reach him?"

"It may be deep out there." Penny could see how high the water came on the trees beside the fallen one. "But ponies can swim," she added. She hadn't the slightest idea how she would manage to swim with Kim if the need arose. She used her heels to make Kim go deeper into the water. He stopped once and she dug her heels into his sides and gave him a tap with her whip.

Slowly he went on. Penny hoped there were no deep holes he might stumble into, and curled her feet back to keep them dry, for the water was up to the girths. She had less control over Kim like that but she made him go on, and she reached the tree.

"Is he all right?" called Joanna.

"I think so," Penny called back, as Gay sat up, timid and shivering. Penny spoke to her gently. "Good little dog!" Gay's tail flickered very slightly.

Penny had difficulty in making Kim come up beside the tree. The water was deep there and it reached the edge of the saddle flaps. Penny gave up trying to keep her feet dry. Every time she tried to reach Gay Kim sidled away. She kicked her heels into him. "Get up, Kim," she said sharply.

He decided he must do as she wished and stood quietly alongside the tree trunk. It had fallen across another tree and lay at an angle, its branches a tangled mass in the water.

Penny reached out to Gay, who lay cowering, and spoke to her reassuringly. "Good dog! There's a good dog! Come on, poodle, then."

Her fingers tightened on the scruff of Gay's

neck and she began to lift her. Gay tried to cling to the tree trunk with her paws and nails, for she was afraid of the water and scared by all her experiences, but Penny lifted her firmly and swung her across on to the saddle in front of her.

"You poor little thing! You are wet and cold," she said. "Poor wee poodle!" Penny loved animals and understood them, and Gay felt confidence in her at once. Holding Gay close to her Penny began to walk Kim slowly back to dry land. He was only too anxious to get there and she had to hold him in to make him go slowly. She was afraid of him plunging into a hole or uneven ground, and she didn't want to risk a spill and dropping the poodle. Also, when he hurried he splashed quite a lot, and Penny didn't want to get any wetter.

"Good boy, Kim. You didn't want to go in but you did!" Penny said as they came out on the bank, where Joanna was waiting axiously.

"Is he all right?" she asked.

Penny dropped the reins on Kim's neck, and he immediately put his head down to crop grass. She fondled Gay and held her up to look at her.

"No wounds or broken bones as far as I can see. It's a she and quite young, she hasn't lost all her puppy coat. She's very wet and cold and scared."

"Oh, I am glad she's all right," Joanna said. "I wonder how she got there."

"I should think she's lost. Look Jo, I want to wrap her in my jacket. Can you get off and hold her while I take it off?"

Joanna dismounted and looped Twinkle's reins over her wrist, then she took Gay in her arms and talked to her, rubbing her cheek against the top of Gay's head while Penny took off her coat. Gay lay still; she was beginning to feel reassured by Penny and Joanna, whose kindness was so like Bridget's and Robin's. Penny wrapped her in the coat and tucked her under her arm. She picked up her reins, dragged Kim away from the grass he was enjoying and said, "We must get her home as quickly as we can and dry her or she'll get a chill, or pneumonia. I can manage her all right as long as she keeps still, and she doesn't seem very lively."

They cantered to the end of the field and Joanna and Twinkle opened the gate.

"You are wet, Penny!" Joanna said, as they turned into the road towards their home.

Penny's jodhpurs were soaked from the knees down. "We'll soon be home," she said, "and then I can change, but this poodle is much more urgent than me."

"Can you trot carrying her?"

"It's not as easy as cantering and rather uncomfortable for her, but we can jog along, it's not far now," Penny replied. "What a good thing we came this way instead of going the long way round!"

"All because I wanted to see a kingfisher! And I nearly didn't see her," said Joanna. "It was only the last minute before we came away from the river I saw something white. Do you know, I thought it was a sheet of paper at first. Then I looked again. I nearly didn't."

"Thank goodness you did! I think she'd have died of cold if she'd been left there much longer. She must have been too tired to swim back. She seemed just limp and done in."

"Does she seem all right?" asked Joanna.

Penny looked down at the bundle under her arm. "She's awfully still, with her eyes shut," she said anxiously.

"I do hope she recovers," said Joanna. "I say, Penny, what'll the Skoot Poot say?"

"Oh gosh! She'll be furious at a poodle coming into the house. She'll jolly well have to lump it!"

"We can keep this poodle, can't we?" asked Joanna.

"Well, I suppose the owner will come and claim it," Penny said.

"I hope they don't," said Joanna. "They can't care for her much to let her get lost like that."

"It may not have been their fault," said Penny. "Dogs do rush away if they're frightened. I hope she'll be all right, she might get a bad chill."

They reached a village and turned in at a gate leading to a small house. Joanna slipped off Twinkle. "Shall I take her?" she said.

Penny handed down the bundle of hacking jacket with Gay's head peeping out. Joanna took it very carefully and Penny jumped off Kim.

"Will you turn Kim out for me, Jo? I want to take her in and get her something warm to drink as quickly as I can."

"O.K." Joanna would have liked to help, but she saw that it would save time if she took Kim for Penny.

Penny went in by the back door, calling "Mummie! Mummie!" and found her mother, Mrs. Maitland, in the kitchen preparing tea.

"Hello, darling! Did you have a nice ride? What have you got there?"

"A poodle. We found her," Penny told her

mother briefly as she put the coat down by the kitchen stove.

Mrs. Maitland came and bent down over her.

"Poor little scrap! She looks absolutely done in. Warm milk with some brandy in it, I think. I'll get some."

"Oh thank you, Mummie." Penny knelt on the floor beside Gay until her mother came back. "She's awfully cold, Mummie, she's drier but she's cold when you touch her. Wet dogs generally steam with warmth."

Mrs. Maitland felt her. "Yes, she is cold. She may have been lying there, wet, for some time. I think she's suffering from exhaustion. Perhaps she's been lost for several days and wandering round without food and then she collapsed."

She offered Gay a saucer of warm milk and Gay lapped a little.

"Has it got brandy in it?" asked Penny.

"No. I didn't think she'd take it and I wanted her to drink all she would. We'll give her a spoonful with brandy now."

Penny skilfully made a pouch of Gay's lip, Mrs. Maitland slipped in a spoonful and Penny stroked Gay's throat. They were experts with sick animals.

"She's swallowing it," Penny said.

"Good. We'll give her that every two hours until she's stronger. It had glucose in it and that's strengthening."

Penny looked at Gay's feet.

"Her pads look sore and cut, and her nails are very worn down. She must have come miles, Mummie."

"How is she?" asked Joanna, coming in and squatting down beside Gay and Penny.

"Very tired, I think," said Mrs. Maitland, "but with warmth and rest and nourishing food she should soon recover."

"Can we keep her?" asked Joanna.

"No, I'm afraid not, darling. We must tell the police you found her."

"Oh, Mummie! I wish we could keep her."

"But, Joanna, the owner may be miserable because she's lost, and worrying about where she is and what's happening to her," said Mrs. Maitland.

"I know who'll worry about her—the Skoot Poot," said Penny.

"Don't let Scuttle come in here while the puppy's here," Mrs. Maitland said. "She'll be jealous and we don't want the puppy frightened.

Penny, go and change your things, you look wet round the legs."

"I was absolutely soaked. Kim and I dripped water. It was up to his shoulders but he was awfully good."

"Splendid! Run and change before you get a cold. Joanna, will you get a dog basket with a nice cosy cushion? There's a spare one in the attic, and we'll give the puppy a hot water bottle in it and try and get her warmer."

The basket was placed by the stove, the cushion warmed and a hot water bottle put in it wrapped in a piece of old blanket. Then Joanna lifted Gay out of Penny's jacket and laid her in the basket. Gay wriggled down and closed her eyes and gave a little sigh. Mrs. Maitland covered her with another bit of blanket.

"She seems a little warmer; we'll leave her to rest while we have tea. Sleep will do her more good than anything."

Gay snuggled down in the comfortable basket. She was too tired to notice where she was but she knew that these humans were the same sort of people as the Denleys and would treat her well.

The warm milk and brandy had revived her and the heat from the hot water bottle began to warm her chilled little body. She dozed, and when Mrs. Maitland, Penny and Joanna came back later she lapped some warm milk and took another spoonful of brandy and water.

"That's splendid!" said Mrs. Maitland. "She feels warm now and a good night's rest will make a new dog of her!"

"Shall I get up in the night and feed her?" Penny suggested, "and refill her hot bottle?"

"I don't think you need. I'll feed her before I go to bed, quite late, and the kitchen is always warm with the stove burning. You and Joanna can see to her early in the morning."

"We'll get up very early," said Joanna.

"She'll sleep all night and be a good deal better tomorrow, if she escapes catching a chill, and I think she will. You found her just in time."

"I am glad," said Penny.

If she could have spoken Gay would have said the same.

CHAPTER FIVE

GAY MEETS SOME NEW ANIMALS

WHEN Gay woke next morning she felt safe and free from fear for the first time for several days. The chill that had numbed her yesterday had gone, and she was warm in the cosy basket.

She sat up and yawned. The door opened and in came Joanna in pyjamas. She said, "Hello, Poodley! You look better."

Joanna was so like Bridget, who had often come down in her pyjamas to say good morning to Gay and Frills and Fiddle, that Gay smiled. She did this by laying her ears back a little, grinning and showing a welcome in her eyes.

"Poppet!" Joanna said, squatting down beside the basket and stroking her head. She slipped her hand under the blanket. "Quite warm. Good!"

Penny came into the kitchen. "How is she?"

"Better. She was sitting up and she smiled at me. A real poodle smile. She feels warm. No shivers."

Penny felt Gay's nose. "Quite cool," she said. "I

do believe she's none the worse. How marvellous! Let's feed her, she didn't have much last night."

"What'll we give her?" asked Joanna. "A real meal with meat and dog biscuit?"

"I'll ask Mummie," said Penny. "I'll take them up some tea to save Mummie coming down."

She put the kettle on and while she waited for it to boil she knelt beside Gay's basket. "You are a sweetie!" she said; "I wish we could keep you but I don't suppose there's much chance of that. Anyone who lost a darling poodle like you wouldn't stop searching till they found you."

"The police haven't heard of anyone losing a poodle," said Joanna. "Daddy rang them up."

Joanna sat by Gay, stroking her and talking to her, while Penny took up the tea. Gay stretched out one of her forepaws and laid it on Joanna's knee. She liked her. The kitchen was warm and cosy and it all felt like a place where animals were wanted and loved. In fact Gay was going to get quite a surprise when she found how many animals lived there.

"Mummie says a poached egg for the puppy," reported Penny. "Nothing too rich or solid at first. She's awfully glad she's better."

"Bags I poach it!" said Joanna.

Gay enjoyed her egg, with brown bread crumbled into it and moistened with a little milk; she gobbled it up and licked the dish clean.

"She's still hungry, Penny," said Joanna.

"She can have some more later. Mummie said not too much at once in case it upsets her. Let's get dressed and do all the animals and then take her in the garden."

Dressing took three minutes, washing one and hair-brushing one, then they attended to their pets, for there was an unbreakable rule that animals were fed before their owners.

"Now let's take the puppy out in the garden," said Joanna.

"We'd better put her on a lead," suggested Penny. "She doesn't know us and it'd be awful if she ran away."

"I'm sure she wouldn't run away from us," said Joanna, "but still, better be on the safe side." And she put on a collar and lead before taking Gay out.

Gay stepped outside the back door and looked round. She sniffed, quivering and timid; strange places were alarming to her after all her frightening adventures. The garden, like the house, smelt safe and happy. There were lots of new scents and she stepped out to investigate. Joanna took her for a little stroll round the lawn and then put her back in her basket in the kitchen.

Mrs. Maitland came down and was very pleased to find Gay so much better.

"I think she ought to be a semi-invalid today," she said, "to give her time to get over it all; we don't know what she's been through and she's only a puppy. Rest today with several light meals."

"She ate her breakfast as if she was hungry," Penny said.

"That's good. Get ready for breakfast, you two."

"We are," said Joanna.

"Indeed you're not!" smiled Mrs. Maitland. "Go and get tidy. You look as if you dressed in a hurry!"

Gay spent the morning dozing. She was still tired and ready to sleep, but after a lunch of brown bread and gravy, and a little meat, she felt more energetic and left her basket to explore the kitchen.

"Have you come here to stay?" asked a voice above her head. Looking up Gay saw a large ginger cat sitting on the window sill. He had a long, fine coat and was a rich orange colour; he was very handsome and he knew it.

Neither the Denleys nor the Masons had kept a cat so Gay had never seen one very close to her and she began to bark.

"Don't make that noise," said the cat. "I don't like it."

Gay stopped barking and sat down, looking up at him.

"If you're going to stay here, you'll have to be polite to me," said the cat. "I'm just as important as any dog and much wiser. You won't get the better of me!"

"Of course not," Gay said politely.

"And no chasing me, because I won't have it. I'll scratch! I'm not a common sort of cat. My name's Stalky and my mother was Rikki Tikki, we're very special cats. What are you doing here?"

Gay told him.

"I might have guessed you were another stray," Stalky said contemptuously. "Those girls are always finding some animal that's been stupid enough to get into trouble." He stood up and stretched, waited a minute to give Gay time to admire him, and then sprang down into the garden.

Gay went back to her basket wondering what other animals she would meet; the garden had been full of strange scents. In the afternoon Joanna took her out and let her lie on her lap in the sun where she dozed contentedly. She had a little walk round the garden and then went indoors again.

Tea, supper, bed-time—the time passed quickly and Gay was rapidly regaining her strength.

The next morning Gay was feeling herself again. She ran about the garden when Joanna took her out before breakfast and was quite lively.

"Bother school!" Joanna said, at breakfast. "I'd like to play with the puppy, she was quite frisky!"

"Much better not get fond of her," said Mr. Maitland. "Her owner may turn up to fetch her any day."

"They don't deserve her! If they cared for her they'd have traced her by now," Joanna said.

"It does seem odd that they haven't," said Mrs. Maitland. "Now the police know she's here you'd think the owner would have heard. They're sure to come, so don't count on keeping her, Joanna."

"I do wish she was mine!" sighed Joanna.

"It's time you started for school and I got off to the office," Mr. Maitland said, looking at his watch.

After a little chivvying by Mrs. Maitland and some hurried searching for missing belongings, Penny and Joanna left for school and Gay stayed with Mrs. Maitland.

At first she lay in her basket while Mrs. Maitland washed up the breakfast things. Then she got out and looked for something to play with.

"You certainly are better!" Mrs. Maitland said, seeing her chewing the corner of the floor rug. She found her a bone to gnaw and it kept Gay quiet for quite a long time, until she became tired of it and looked round for something else to do. Mrs. Maitland went out by the back door to fetch something and Gay trotted out too.

She stopped dead. A white poodle was lying on the path, enjoying the sun. When she saw Gay she said:

"So it's you who's in the kitchen! And I'm kept out. What are you doing here, anyway?"

"I got lost and they brought me here," said Gay apologetically.

"As long as you don't think you're the favourite dog—because I am—I don't mind you staying," said the other poodle. "But you're not to sit on my Missus' lap. You can have Penny and Joanna, but Missus is mine!"

Gay sat down in the sun. She stretched out her forepaws and then crossed one over the other.

"I'm glad you're a real poodle and cross your paws; other dogs can't do it properly. We poodles must stick together and keep that spaniel, Peter Popples, in his place. A very common dog!"

Mrs. Maitland looked out of the back door. "Oh!

There you are, puppy, I had quite a fright when I found you'd gone out. You seem to have settled down there and the sun will do you good. Now, Scuttle, you're not to be cross or jealous. Be good to the puppy, Scuttle!"

Scuttle looked up with a smiling expression and thumped her tail on the path.

"Oh, I know you can look as if butter wouldn't melt in your mouth but I know how wicked you can be!" said Mrs. Maitland sternly. "Still, if Scoot's made friends they'll be all right together."

She looked to see if the gate into the road was shut and decided to leave the back door open so that the puppy could run indoors if she wanted to, she was afraid that if anything startled her Gay might panic and run away. She looked out several times and saw the poodles lying side by side. She thought how nice they looked, the puppy was a dear little dog, and she wished they could keep her.

Scuttle told Gay that she'd been with the Maitlands all her life, three years. "They're the best family in the world except for having too many pets. I don't like sharing with a lot of animals."

Just then a lemon and white cocker spaniel looked round the corner of the house and then bounced up to them.

"Hullo! You're new," he said to Gay; he sniffed and blew at her, wagging his tail.

Gay retreated a little.

"Try and behave like a gentleman, even if you aren't one, Peter," said Scuttle. "Don't puff at her in that vulgar way, and keep those great ears from flapping about so, they make a draught."

"Sorry!" Peter said, "nothing I do is ever right with you."

"That's your bad manners," said Scuttle, "but we don't expect much from a spaniel."

Peter smacked one of his fore paws at Gay in an attempt at play, sank down on his front legs and said "Woof!"

Gay, on her dignity and a little timid of him, snapped gently to show she wasn't ready to play till she knew him better.

"Quite right, don't encourage him. The clumsy great thing," said Scuttle. "You and I'll play when we want to. Look out, here's Jack. Don't stand any nonsense from him."

Looking round Gay saw a black bird, a tame jackdaw, hopping along the path.

He said "Jack. Good boy Peter." He barked like a dog. "I am clever. Ha ha! Scoot! Scoot!"

"Go away and be quiet," growled Scuttle.

Jack hopped round her, his head on one side as he watched her with his bright, mischievous eyes. "Scoot Poot! Scoot Poot! Ha ha!" he said.

"Shut up!" Scuttle growled.

Jack turned quickly and Gay saw Stalky watching him, his tail twitching.

"You'll catch it if you touch him," said Scuttle. "I wish you would though!"

Mrs. Maitland came out of the house and the animals all gazed into the distance as if they hadn't seen each other.

"Jack, don't tease the dogs," she said. "You'd better go in your cage before you get into mischief. Stalky, you look too good to be true! What are you up to?"

Stalky purred and miaoued as he rubbed against her. She shut Jack in a large cage which was built round a tree, then she took Gay in to have her lunch.

In the afternoon Gay went out with Scuttle who took her round the garden. Scuttle showed Gay the best grass for eating, a tree which Stalky could easily be chased up, and took her down to the end of the garden where a gate led into a paddock.

Kim and Twinkle were grazing there, and when Scuttle barked at them they trotted up to the gate.

"Thank you for rescuing me the other day," Gay said.

"I wouldn't have if Penny hadn't made me," Kim replied. "Where are they today?"

"School," said Scuttle.

Twinkle snorted. "Children must be the stupidest creatures! They're always having to go back to be schooled; we are broken in and then we're finished, except for some schooling for something special, but children must forget it at once because they have to go back for schooling!"

"And then they come home, having left us for ages, and say we're fat and start exercising us," said Kim. He nibbled some grass. "Still, the children here are all right, they do consider us. Not like some."

"They're the best in the world," said Scuttle fiercely. "I'll nip you if you don't think so too!"

"Oh, I do! I do!" Twinkle said. "Don't come round my heels, you make me nervous, and then I might kick you."

"You dare!" Scuttle growled. "Come on, Poodle. You've met everyone now except Jenny."

"What's that?"

"You'll soon see. One of Penny's pets. The worst of the lot."

CHAPTER SIX

WHO WILL CLAIM HER?

JUST before tea-time there was suddenly a lot of noise in the house. Doors banged, footsteps ran upstairs and then clattered down again, there was a lot of chattering and Scuttle barked excitedly. Peter rushed into the kitchen and gambolled round madly. Gay got into her basket, she already felt it was her own place where she was safe.

The children had come home from school. They came to see Gay and petted her, asking how she'd been all day. Gay felt so happy at being treated as a dog who was wanted and loved again that she couldn't bear to think of the time she'd spent at the Masons'.

After tea Penny said, "Come on, Jo, let's go to the ponies, there's a little time before it'll be dark."

They ran down to the paddock to ride Kim and Twinkle bare-back for a short while. Gay followed them and watched, sitting by the gate with Peter, who occasionally galumphed about the paddock getting in the way and wagging his tail with great enthusiasm when Joanna or Peter yelled, "Look out, Pete!"

Soon it began to get dark and Penny called, "We'd better go and do all the animals, Joanna."

"And homework. Bother it!" Joanna dismounted and took off Twinkle's bridle.

"Supper!" Peter wagged his tail. "They always feed us before they have theirs."

"Of course," said Kim, looking over the gate. "All the best people do and Penny and Joanna are absolutely best."

Penny and Joanna had quite a lot of work in keeping their pets clean and fed. When they had attended to them they went indoors and Joanna took Gay's basket into the dining-room where the girls were to do their homework.

Then Gay saw a curious little white animal. She took a step towards it and growled.

"No, quiet. You must be friends with Jenny," Penny said.

The white animal, which had red eyes and a long tail, ran up Penny's arm and sat on her shoulder. Gay watched it with great curiosity. She had never seen an ordinary rat, far less a tame, white rat. Jenny ran about the room while the children did their homework. Penny kept a cautious eye on Gay in case she snapped, but she sat in her basket watching Jenny, who ran about the room, up the curtains, down on to the sideboard to investigate the dishes there and then up the table leg to scamper about among the lesson books strewn over it.

"Go away, Jenny," said Joanna; "keep off my arithmetic, you'll smudge it."

"Hey! Jenny! Don't drink the ink!" cried Penny. Jenny ran up Penny's arm and sat on her shoulder, where she sat up and cleaned her white coat by licking it all over. Then she licked her long tail, holding it in her front paws which she used just like hands. She went over every inch of her tail, then she combed her whiskers with her claws and sat up on her hind legs. Penny got up to fetch a book and Jenny remained upright on her shoulder, holding on to Penny's ear with one paw. suddenly she leapt down, on to the table, across it like a flash and down on to the floor.

"No, poodle, no," Penny said warningly, seeing Gay quiver with excitement.

Mrs. Maitland came in to lay supper.

"Oh, Mummie, don't leave the door open,

please," Penny said quickly. "Stalky might come in and Jenny's loose."

"I can't believe Jenny is a help with homework," said Mrs. Maitland, shutting the door. "Have you finished?"

"I know as much French verbs as I ever will," Joanna said, shutting her book. "I wonder if poodles know them, they're French dogs!" She sat down by Gay and took her on her lap.

Penny put Jenny back in her cage while they had supper, Mrs. Maitland having, not unreasonably, said Jenny must not attend their meals.

"No one has rung up or come about the puppy," Mrs. Maitland said, as they sat down to supper.

"Perhaps we'll be able to keep her," said Joanna.

"How smashing if we can!" Penny said. "I wish we knew what she's called."

"We could try some names on her," Mr. Maitland said, "and see if she answers. Rover! Fido!"

Of course Gay took no notice.

"Daddy! Those aren't poodle sort of names!" Joanna said.

Mrs. Maitland suggested Candy, Lucy, Suzette, Fifi and Mitzi.

Penny and Joanna tried Snowy, Prue, Tess, Muffin, Topsy and Wistful.

Mr. Maitland thought of Lulu and Cracker and Tinkerbell.

Still Gay took no notice at all.

"We might never think of it if she's got an unusual name," said Mrs. Maitland.

"She ought to have something that sounds jolly," said Penny. "She was so gay in the garden."

"She looked up when you said gay!" exclaimed Joanna.

"Gay! Gay!" called Penny and the puppy got up and trotted across to her.

"That's it! What a nice name!" said Mrs. Maitland.

"Gay, come here," said Mr. Maitland.

Gay went round to him; she stood up and put her paws on his knee, looking up at him and wagging her tail. It was nice that they were going to use her name that she knew well, instead of calling her Poodle or Puppy.

"That's it all right," Mr. Maitland said. "Now we ought to find her owner."

"Oh no, Daddy!" cried Joanna.

"Don't let's try too hard," said Penny.

"I don't want you to get fond of her and then have to give her up," he said, "because someone's sure to claim her some time."

Gay settled down with the Maitlands. She played with Peter Popples, racing round the lawn with Peter galloping after her, tripping over his great paws as he tried to turn and dodge as quickly as Gay. She and Scuttle played too, but Scuttle didn't like it if Peter joined in. Gay cheeked Stalky and, with Scuttle egging her on, chased him up the tree sometimes. She went to say good morning to the ponies every day, and she became used to Jenny, but she was afraid of hurting her and would quiver with anxiety when Jenny came close to her. Jack learnt to call "Gay!" in a voice like Penny's. He would wait till Gay was asleep in the sun and then call her. Gay would jump up and look round, when Jack would cackle with laughter. But it was Joanna whom Gay liked best.

One evening Mrs. Maitland was sitting in the kitchen, in a comfy old easy chair; she was mending Joanna's jodhpurs for her to ride in next day, the three dogs were asleep on the rug in front of the stove and Stalky was curled up in a chair. Penny and Joanna had just finished their homework and come into the kitchen, Jenny riding on Penny's shoulder.

"No one's come to claim Gay," Mrs. Maitland said. "She's been here two weeks."

"I hope nobody comes," said Joanna.

"Quite one of the family, aren't you, Gay?" Mrs. Maitland said, patting her. Gay stood up and put her paws on Mrs. Maitland's knee.

Scuttle leapt up and galloped across the room growling. "Don't you dare get on her lap. It's mine. That's my Missus. I won't let anyone else sit on her lap!"

"Be quiet, Scuttle, don't growl like that," said Mrs. Maitland. "You mustn't be so jealous."

"Cross little Scoot!" said Penny.

"Horrid, jealous Scoodle-Poodle!" Joanna said, picking up Gay and petting her.

"She's a one-man dog," Mrs. Maitland said, apologizing for her. "She's devoted to me and doesn't care for anyone else. I believe she'd do anything for me."

"Course I would," growled Scuttle. "I'd die or give up my best bone for my Missus. Go away, Gay, don't come near her." Scuttle had scrambled on to Mrs. Maitland's lap and sat there growling defiantly.

"You're sitting on Scuttle's Collection, Mummie; she collects things and puts them in that chair and they fall down in the springs where it's bust," said Penny.

"She takes things of mine if I go out and leave her," said Mrs. Maitland. "Is this where she puts them?" She put her hand down into the old chair and drew out one of her own gloves. Next came some chewed paper, then one of her stockings, an old dry bone and lastly a ball of wool. "I wondered where that glove and the wool had got to," said Mrs. Maitland. "I'll look in Scoot's Collection next time I miss anything."

"You're a sweetie, Gay!" said Joanna. "Isn't she, Mum?"

"Yes, but I'm afraid she's a little thief," Mrs. Maitland said. "I bought half a dozen buns this afternoon, those sticky sugary ones you like, and left them in the bag on the table. They all disappeared. Scuttle was with me and Peter was out with Daddy, so I'm afraid it must have been Gay. Of course, she's young, but she must learn not to steal food. We can't scold her unless we catch her taking something, so we must watch her."

"Oh Gay, how awful!" said Joanna. "Didn't anyone tell you how naughty it is to steal buns?"

"Jenny was out all the afternoon," Penny said. "I was cleaning and airing her cage. She was loose for quite a long time. She's an awful little thief."

"I don't think she could carry such big buns," said Mrs. Maitland.

"If she took them she'd hide them," said Penny. "She always does."

Later in the evening Penny saw Peter sniffing at the door of the cupboard under the stairs.

"What's up, Pete? What's in there?"

Peter wagged his tail and snuffed at the door, which was ajar. Penny opened it and Peter went in and sniffed about.

"Lend me your torch, Joanna?" asked Penny. "Peter Popples has got something in here."

"A mouse perhaps." Joanna flashed her torch in the cupboard. At the end of the cupboard, under the bottom step of the stairs, were six buns in a row.

"The buns!" cried Joanna. "It wasn't Gay who took them."

"It was Jenny," Penny agreed. "That's just the sort of place she'd hide them in."

"Fancy her carrying them so far," said Mrs. Maitland. "I'd like to have seen her getting them down from the table, it must have been quite a job for her. Jenny always stores what she steals; do you remember when she took my tulip bulbs and hid them in my desk?"

"What shall we do with the buns?" asked Penny. "Pete's eating one!"

"Let them have them. They're no use now," Mrs. Maitland said. "Don't forget it's Guy Fawkes Day next week. All the animals must be shut in so they aren't frightened, or they might run away and get hurt."

"None of ours are going to get hurt," Penny declared. "We'll bring them all into the kitchen and turn the wireless on so loud they don't hear any bangs!"

"A good idea," said Mrs. Maitland, "but not for the ponies. I don't want Kim and Twinkle listening to the wireless in the kitchen."

Penny and Joanna laughed. "I'm sure they'd behave beautifully," said Penny, "but we'll put them in the stables. Kim doesn't need any excuse for getting out of the field."

"You shan't be frightened by fireworks," Joanna said to Gay. "You're a beautiful poodle. A boofle-poofle!"

Gay laid her head on Joanna's shoulder, blissfully happy at being one of such a nice family. She had given up thinking about Barbara Mason; she was quite sure that she belonged to the Maitlands now.

CHAPTER SEVEN

"IT WASN'T TWINKLE'S FAULT"

JOANNA sat on the manger in the stable talking to Twinkle, who was nudging her with his nose in the hopes of getting some more sugar.

"It's no use, Twink, you've eaten it all." Joanna stroked his muzzle and put her face down against it; he was so soft and warm and he smelt nice. His shaggy winter coat made him look as if he was wearing a fur coat, she thought. In winter he was almost black and in summer he was a dark, glossy brown.

She was waiting for Penny, who had gone on an errand for Mrs. Maitland; when she came back they were going for a ride. Joanna didn't mind waiting with Twinkle because she was one of those people who like having a pony and being with him almost as much as riding him; she was always happy just pottering about with her animals, but Penny liked riding and jumping and gymkhanas best.

"Sorry to be so long." Penny's face appeared over the half-door. "Oh, I thought you'd have got the ponies ready."

"I caught Kim when I got Twinkle." Joanna got down from the manger. Together they fetched saddles and bridles and Penny grumbled that the afternoons were short in winter. "Though we're lucky to have a fine Saturday, considering what a lot it's rained lately."

"Where shall we go?" Joanna asked, as they went out of the gate. Twinkle was pleased to be going out, he was playing with his bit and kept breaking into a little jiggly trot.

"Along by the river and back across the fields? Then we can have a gallop." Penny let Kim trot and they went down the road towards the river.

"No poodle today, and no kingfisher," Joanna said, when they rode along by the water. "Oh, I do hope no one comes and claims Gay."

"I shouldn't think anyone would now," replied Penny. "We've had her several weeks, but I wish she wasn't so scared of going outside the garden. She's full of go at home but she's terribly timid anywhere else. Bags open this gate. I want to get Kim really good at it in case there are some Hunter Trials we could go in for in the Easter hols."

"I think he is good at them already," Joanna said, as she watched them open the gate. Kim knew all about it and pushed with his chest at just the right moment and turned and waited while Penny shut it. Joanna knew she'd never do it as well as that, or make Twinkle into such an expert. They left the river and cantered up a long slope, then Penny and Kim went ahead across the big field, with Kim's hooves squelching in the wet ground and throwing up little bits of muddy turf. Joanna and Twinkle came along behind, for Twinkle was smaller and not as fast as Kim, and Joanna didn't hurry him unduly.

"Oh blow!" Penny exclaimed, when she pulled up at the end of the field and saw the gate into the next one. "It's off its hinges, we'll never be able to open it."

"It's tied up with wire," Joanna pointed out; "to keep it together till it's mended, I expect."

Penny looked round. "What a swizz if we can't go that way. And Mr. Anderson said we could ride here."

"If we shut gates," said Joanna.

"We can't open this one, let alone shut it. Look, Jo, there's a very low place in the fence. Can you jump it?"

Joanna looked at it doubtfully. She quite liked going over the jumps in their field but she always thought strange ones were difficult and looked bigger than they were. Still, if Penny was keen on going home that way she supposed she must try. "All right. I expect we can."

"Of course you can. Twinkle jumps awfully well and it's really quite low. I'll give you a lead."

Kim jumped readily and cleared the fence with plenty to spare, and Joanna wished she could jump like that, easily and without wondering if she was going to get over all right. Penny had pulled up and was looking back to watch her jump.

She shortened her reins and touched Twinkle with her heels. He needed no urging to join Kim and he went faster than Joanna wanted him to, she'd no time to steady him before he took off. She had a glimpse of the hedge below her as he sailed over it, and then as he landed he seemed to slide and then he was down on the ground on his side and she was rolling over with Twinkle struggling to get up and nearly treading on her.

Penny was off Kim in a minute and she ran to see if Joanna was hurt. "Are you all right?"

"Yes, I think so." Joanna was determined not to

cry but her lip wobbled. "I bumped my face."

"Yes, you've grazed your cheek badly, on a stone I expect. Nothing else, Jo?"

"No. Is Twink all right?" Joanna got to her feet slowly.

Penny caught Twinkle, who was grazing near, led him back to Joanna and looked him over. "He's O.K. No cuts and he's sound. I oughtn't to have jumped with the ground so wet and slippery, only I didn't think of it. I'm sorry, Jo, it wasn't Twinkle's fault. Or yours. It was mine."

Joanna took Twinkle's reins. The idea of getting on again didn't appeal to her but her legs felt rather shaky so it might be easier to ride than to stand. Slowly she mounted and tried not to feel she wanted to hold on to the mane.

Penny caught Kim, who was taking the opportunity to eat as much grass as possible. "Sure you're all right, Jo? We'll go home slowly, and everyone says it's best to get on again at once after a fall. Then you don't lose your nerve."

As they walked the ponies across to the next gate, which led into a lane and would take them home quite quickly, Joanna thought that she'd never had much nerve when it came to jumping, and now she'd lost it all, because if a pony could fall down, just like that, she didn't think she'd want to jump again.

"It would have been awful if Twinkle had been hurt. If he'd broken a leg or something," she said.

"Awful," agreed Penny, looking at her and thinking that she was very pale. "It's lucky the ground's so soft. I'm sorry, Jo, I was an idiot not to think that it was too slippery to be safe. People put special studs in their horses' shoes for jumping when the ground's wet and slippery."

"It doesn't matter as long as Twink's all right," Joanna said, though her cheek was getting stiff and was throbbing painfully.

It seemed a long way home. They walked most of the way and trotted slowly, and Joanna was very glad when they reached home and she could slide off Twinkle and let Penny take him to turn him out, while she went indoors.

"I am sorry, darling," said Mrs. Maitland, when Joanna had told her what had happened. "You've got a nasty bump and graze on your cheek. We'll bathe it. Does your head ache?"

"A bit."

"I should go up and lie down. It's a good plan after a tumble. I'll bring you a hot water bottle and a cup of tea."

"Thank you. I'll take Gay up with me. Has she been good?"

"Very good. But I tried to take her out for a little walk and she was so frightened when we got out into the road that I had to bring her back."

"Poor Gay!"

"Yes, she hasn't forgotten whatever it was that happened to her when she was lost, she's very timid of strange places and strange people. I wish we could get her over it."

Snuggling down under her eiderdown with Gay cuddling up against her, Joanna whispered, "I know how you feel, Gay, when you're scared of going out, because I feel scared of riding now. I don't want to ride again."

CHAPTER EIGHT

GAY AND TWINKLE ARE FRIENDS

"IT'S such a waste," said Penny. "Twinkle's a super pony and he jumps awfully well but she just doesn't ride him."

"Don't try and persuade her to," Mrs. Maitland said. "People often lose their nerve after a fall and I'm sure she'll get over it in time, but not if she's made to ride before she feels ready to."

"She's perfectly happy messing about with Twinkle, grooming him and leading him about and giving him much too much sugar." Penny was helping her mother get tea ready and she put the tea cups on a tray. "And Gay follows Joanna and Twinkle everywhere, those three are terrific pals."

"Gay and Joanna are a pair!" said Penny. And she began to wonder again how she could help Joanna to get over the effect of her fall. She enjoyed riding and jumping so much herself that she wanted Joanna to enjoy it too; besides, she thought that Jo would be growing too big for Twinkle in time, so it was a a pity to waste time while she had him.

"Kim's going like a bomb!" she said. "I'm sure he'll do well in the Hunter Trials. It is a pity that Joanna's gone off riding, she's going to miss such a lot of fun."

"Don't fuss her about it," Mrs. Maitland advised. "Would you tell her it's time she came in to tea?"

Penny went out and found Joanna had Twinkle in the garden and was letting him eat some grass growing on a rough bank. "It's got clover in it and he's enjoying it."

"It's tea-time."

"Bother! That's all for today, Twink." She persuaded him to leave the grass and led him back towards the gate into the field. Gay trotted beside them.

"Mummie says she can't get Gay to go out of the garden," Penny said. "Couldn't you train her to?"

"Me? You'd do it better than I should, Penny. Anyhow, what's it matter? She's quite happy in the garden." Joanna opened the gate and led Twinkle through.

"Look what fun she's missing. Walks with Peter and Scuttle, and we won't be able to take her when we go for picnics in the summer if she's scared to go out of the garden. Scuttle loves going, especially if we go to the sea."

Joanna took off the halter and gave Twinkle a pat. Scuttle did love going out in the car for a picnic, and she liked the sea too. What Penny had said was right. Gay would miss a lot of fun if she wouldn't go out anywhere, and they couldn't leave her alone when they all went out, she'd hate that. Somehow she'd got to get her used to it. She thought about it all that evening and by the time she went to bed she thought she'd hit on a way to cure Gay's shyness.

Squatting down on the floor beside Gay's basket in the kitchen she told her, "You didn't mind coming here on Kim because he saved you from the river. And he brought you here, which you like, so you know that ponies are all right. And Twinkle and you are friends. Perhaps if you went out on the road on Twinkle at first you wouldn't be scared." Joanna gave Gay a kiss on the top of her head where it was curly. "We'll try, Gay, and perhaps when you're used to it you can go out on a lead like Scoot does." Another kiss—"Good night, sweetie. We'll try tomorrow."

As she lay in bed Joanna thought, "I've got to

ride Twinkle to take Gay out. But I'll only be walking about on him, and it's not as bad for me as it is for Gay. Only I wish it didn't get dark so early; there's only week-ends to do much in."

On the next Saturday Penny was surprised and pleased to find Joanna riding Twinkle slowly round the paddock carrying Gay in front of her. "Giving Gay a ride?" Penny asked. She wasn't going to make any comment on Joanna riding again in case it put her off.

Joanna explained her plan to Penny. "Do you think it'll work?"

"Yes, it might. You'll have to be careful she doesn't struggle and jump down when you first go out on the road."

"Could you lead Twinkle so I've both hands to hold her?"

"Yes, of course I will."

"We won't be ready yet. I thought I'd make her absolutely used to it before we go out of the field and garden."

"Yes, that'd be best, don't hurry it," Penny said, and she thought that Joanna couldn't have found a better way of overcoming her own nervousness; sitting on Twinkle and ambling about with Gay she'd soon forget her fears, only she wouldn't say so. Jo was doing it for Gay and that was the best way.

Every week-end, and on week-days if they got home from school early, Joanna rode about with Gay in front of her on the saddle. Gay seemed to like it and leaned against Joanna with complete confidence. Penny declared that Gay had the oddest seat on a horse that she'd ever seen, "the opposite to the forward seat!" Gay learnt to jump on to Joanna's knees from a high bank and Penny remarked it was lucky that Twinkle was so quiet.

"He's an angel!" Joanna kissed the smooth bit on his forehead where there was a white star. Gay looked up at him and wagged her tail. "She's saying thank you," said Joanna. "She loves Twinkle." With Gay jumping up to lick her hand and Twinkle resting his head on her shoulder or trying to get his nose into her pocket to search for sugar, Joanna was blissfully happy. Twinkle followed her about without a head collar, just as closely as Gay did, and though Mr. Maitland sometimes complained about hoofmarks on the lawn, and Twinkle occasionally ate some choice plant, nobody really minded her bringing him into the garden.

When the children were at school Gay often went down to the field for a chat with the ponies. Twinkle was her special friend.

"I couldn't help slipping up that day," Twinkle said. "I wouldn't fall with Joanna or Penny for a sack of oats. Since then she hasn't taken me out anywhere and it's dull staying in the field always. I'd like to take her for a good gallop."

So when Joanna rode out into the road soon after this Gay was thinking that Twinkle would be pleased, and she forgot about being scared of going outside the garden, nor did she notice that Joanna was holding her very carefully and that Penny was walking by Twinkle.

"It's going to work, I really think it is," said Joanna. "She isn't a bit scared or taking any notice of anything. We'll come out again this afternoon, and twice tomorrow. She'll soon be used to it and then she can come on a lead. Perhaps I'll carry her for a bit the first time. Isn't it lucky Twinkle's so good, and such friends with Gay? He wouldn't do anything to scare her."

When they went home and dismounted Gay stood up on her hind legs to sniff at Twinkle's nose. "She's thanking him," Joanna said delightedly. "Twinkle's going to cure her of nervousness."

Penny thought that Gay and Twinkle would cure Joanna, but she only said, "Keep it up."

The day she was late and trotted all the way home, after taking Gay further than usual, was a big step forward. A little later Penny remarked that cantering was easier than trotting for Gay, "not so joggly for her," and Joanna took Gay for a canter round the field.

"She's cured, Mummie," said Penny. "All except for jumping and we can't expect Gay to do that!"

"She'll decide she wants to presently," said Mrs. Maitland.

"She never was terribly keen, and I can't see what there is to make her want to start again."

"Leave it to Gay!" smiled Mrs. Maitland. "She's improving fast. She came out in the car and enjoyed it yesterday."

"Gay's ready to go out on a lead," Joanna announced soon after this. "Will you bring Scuttle and Peter? She'll be better with them there too."

"Walkies!" said Penny, and Scuttle and Peter bounced about excitedly until Penny put on their leads. Joanna was putting a collar and lead on Gay, who shivered a little with excitement. "Come on, Gay, walkies!"

When they reached the gate Joanna watched Gay; before she'd always crouched down and refused to follow, no amount of coaxing had got her out into the road, but now she was walking beside Scuttle with her tail up and looking quite happy.

"My plan's worked," cried Joanna.

"It was a jolly good idea," Penny said. "She's enjoying her walkies as much as Scuttle is. You really did work awfully hard at it."

"It started me riding again too. I don't know when I'd have made myself begin if it hadn't been for wanting to get Gay going out."

"I bet Twinkle's glad, it must be awfully dull for a pony who stays in a field always. You must start jumping again." Penny couldn't help saying it. She was so hoping Joanna would.

"I will some time," was all she said but Penny went on hoping.

Gay had taken to riding so quickly that Joanna thought there must be lots of other things she could teach her. She began by training her to "stay", starting by only going away a few paces and then increasing it. At first Gay got up and followed her, but gradually she learnt until Joanna could go out of sight and Gay would stay where she'd been told till Joanna came back to her. And Gay began to be looked on as Joanna's own dog.

CHAPTER NINE

GAY IN DANGER

NOW that Joanna no longer spent every spare minute in taking Gay out on Twinkle, she and Penny were able to go for rides again at the week-ends and Joanna began to enjoy it again. But she couldn't make herself jump, every time she thought that she really would she found, when she was actually facing the jump, that she couldn't find the courage to put Twinkle over it, no matter how small it was, and she'd say that perhaps she would tomorrow. She despised herself for being a coward and she knew that she wouldn't feel right inside herself until she'd overcome it, but she went on putting it off.

One Saturday afternoon Mr. and Mrs. Maitland went out for a short time, leaving Penny and Joanna at home.

Penny said, "I think we ought to start giving the ponies a feed every day now, as we'll be using them a lot as soon as school breaks up. A small feed as well as their hay would keep them fit, only we don't want to bring them into the stables for it because it takes so long when we've got to get them fed before school. I thought if we had two little wooden boxes they'd do."

"There are lots of old boxes in the shed by the garage, only they're mostly big ones," said Joanna.

"Let's go and see if there's two that would do," said Penny. "If we put their feeds on the ground they'll waste them so."

"Gosh! What awfully junky junk!" said Joanna when they opened the shed door.

"Mummie's always saying this shed's got to be turned out. I expect these old packing cases are for firewood, but if we could find two small ones, not splintery because of their noses——" Penny began to move some of the things which were stacked in the shed. An old fireguard was sticking up at the top of the pile and a tin bath lay on its side with a piece of ragged tennis netting over it.

"Golly! What rubbish! And look at the cobwebs!" Penny pulled a box out of the heap. "It's awfully rocky, it'll topple over if we don't look out."

"It's like playing spillikins!" Joanna extracted a

watering can with a hole in it, and some old tennis rackets began to slide down.

Gay was sniffing round with great interest and Joanna said, "Look out, Gay, something may crash."

"Keep her clear," warned Penny. "These boxes are heavy and if one fell it could crush her. Of course the best ones *would* be at the bottom!" She moved a box and a mouse darted out and scurried across to another box where it disappeared in a crack. Gay dashed after it. Squeezing through the piled up rubbish, she vanished. The box Penny was moving slipped and brought down several others, blocking the gap where Gay had gone in.

"Now she can't get out," cried Joanna, and she knelt down to try and see where Gay was. "I can't see her. Gay! Gay!"

Penny was struggling with a big packing case. "If this comes down too the whole lot may topple over; if she's underneath she'll be crushed. Help me shove it back."

"Oh, it mustn't fall," Joanna cried in great distress. "We must get her out, Penny."

"We can't lift them down, it'd only start them sliding."

They both pushed desperately, and managed to

get the box back on to the pile, which was top-heavy and wobbly. "It'll crash over if I leave go," said Penny.

"What are we to do? We must get her out," said Joanna despairingly. "Could we get someone to lift the things down?"

"We've got to. I can't hold them for ever, and if I let go they'll start sliding and crash." Penny was leaning against the heap and trying to wedge it up. "Can you fetch someone? Fairly quickly?"

Joanna thought hard. "Mr. Parker." He was their nearest neighbour and as he had retired from work he was usually at home. "I'm sure he'd come."

"Phone him, it's quicker," said Penny, leaning hard against the pile. She wasn't sure how long she could hang on for her arms were going to ache.

Joanna ran indoors and looked up the number. If only Mummie or Daddy were at home. What a lot of Parkers. This was him, she dialled the number and heard the telephone ringing at the other end. No reply, he must be in his garden, he was always gardening and Mrs. Parker must be out too. It went on ringing in a hopeless sort of way and she was sure no one was going to answer it. She ran back and told Penny. "I'll fetch him. Can you hang on for a bit?"

"Buck up then, it's jolly heavy."

"I'll be as quick as I can." She'd take Twinkle, riding would be the fastest way of getting there as she could go across two fields, miles quicker than if she went round by road on her bike. The saddle and bridle were down by the gate of the field, as they'd ridden that morning and had left them there in case they rode again, so that saved time.

Twinkle was at the gate too, which was lucky, and thank goodness he was easy to catch. He was saddled and bridled in no time and Joanna led him out and then swung herself into the saddle.

She turned in at the gate and pushed it to close it behind her. Twinkle was quite good at it though not so expert as Kim, probably because she wasn't as expert as Penny was, she thought. Then she set off at a fast canter which soon became a gallop, faster than she'd ever ridden, but with Gay in danger they must hurry.

They crossed the field very quickly and then she saw the *stile*. How could she have forgotten there was a stile between the two fields? It wasn't too big for Twinkle to jump, but Joanna's heart thumped and she felt sick, because she knew she had to jump it. It'd take ages to go back and round by road, and if Penny got tired and couldn't hang on—Joanna had a picture of those heavy boxes sliding down on to Gay. It might kill her, just because Joanna was too much of a coward to jump.

She looked at the stile and set her teeth. No use wasting time sitting looking at it, so she turned Twinkle and trotted him back a little way and then put him at it. No good thinking about how it was solid and wouldn't fall down if he hit it. She'd jumped dozens of times and she knew she could now because Gay depended on it. She found she was doing it all as she'd been taught and without having to think about it, squeeze your legs to send him into his bridle and show him you mean him to jump, grip with your knees and swing forward as he takes off, letting your hands go too. Joanna found she was thinking clearly, and that her frightened, panicky feeling had gone as they sailed over the stile.

Then they were in the next field, and galloping across it and she was shouting aloud, "It's easy!" It was fun too, why on earth had she made a fuss over it?

She clattered up the drive of Mr. Parker's house and looked round. Smoke from a bonfire was curling up at the end of the garden, so she called, "Mr.

Parker," and he came up the path towards her. He was tall and broad, he'd be able to lift heavy boxes.

"Please could you come and help? Quickly. Our poodle's got stuck under some big boxes and they're going to fall on her if someone doesn't help. Penny's holding them up. Please come quickly."

Mr. Parker said "Right." He ran across to the garage and backed his car out, only stopping to call out of the window, "Where is she?"

"In the shed by the garage," shouted Joanna, and then he was gone; the gravel spurted up from under the tyres as he started and she heard him tearing down the road and changing gear, slowing down and hooting at the corner and then racing on. He'd be there in about five minutes, if only Penny was hanging on.

"Twink, you are good!" Joanna said, and hugged his brown, shaggy neck. "And we jumped. I shan't ever mind jumping again."

She cantered back across the field and jumped the stile, just to show herself that she could, and she felt quite pleased when she looked back at it. Really quite a good-sized jump. Good old Twink! Now, if Gay was safe everything would be marvellous!

She saw them outside the garage as she rode in at the gate, Mr. Parker talking to Penny and Gay standing beside them. She was all right. Joanna jumped off and picked Gay up and cuddled her. "Thank you awfully for coming," she said to Mr. Parker.

"Glad to be able to help. Strong girl, Penny, she was hanging on splendidly!"

"I was getting jolly tired, and my arms ached like anything. Thanks a lot for coming so quickly."

When he'd driven away they went to turn Twinkle out and Penny said, "You were jolly quick."

"I went across the fields."

"Over the stile?" Penny asked in surprise. "It's quite a big one."

"Twinkle jumped it superbly. And I jumped it coming back too, just to make sure I didn't really mind."

"Jolly good show," said Penny.

Joanna was taking off Twinkle's saddle and bridle, then he rubbed his head against her and rested it on her shoulder in the way he always did when she petted him. Joanna searched in her pockets and brought out a revolting-looking lump of sugar which was covered in dust and fluff and had several oats sticking to it, along with some bread crumbs. "All I've got," she offered it to Twinkle who seemed to like it. He nodded his head as he ate it and looked round for more but Joanna said, "No more, bad luck Twink," and kissed him on his white star. "He smells awfully nice. Much nicer than people's scent in bottles. Why don't they have Eau de Pony?" Penny giggled. Gay stood up to sniff at Twinkle in a friendly way and then licked Joanna's hand. She'd the two nicest pets in the world.

CHAPTER TEN

EXCITING THINGS

"ARE we going to ride this afternoon?" Joanna asked, one Saturday.

"I can't," Penny answered. "I've got to rehearse." Penny was acting in the end of term play.

"I think I'll go for a little ride and take Gay," Joanna said. "She does love it. And if you can't come it's dull going alone." Besides, she thought, when she and Penny went together they trotted and cantered and galloped because Penny liked a proper ride, but Joanna enjoyed just pottering along, so this was a good day for meandering about with Gay in front of her.

"You're coming riding, not walkies," she told Gay, as they went down to the field. Kim tried to come out too when she brought Twinkle away and nearly trod on her foot. She looked back as she led Twinkle away to get his tack on and hoped that Kim wouldn't break out, he didn't like being left alone and getting out was what he was good at. He put his head down to graze and she thought he'd be all right.

She brushed the dry mud off Twinkle and saddled and bridled him. Gay sat watching, she knew perfectly what was coming, and when Joanna mounted she got up on the bank and waited for Joanna to bring Twinkle up beside it, then she jumped across on to the front of the saddle and sat there, leaning back against Joanna and perfectly at ease, and Joanna kept her arms round her.

"Which way shall we go?" Joanna asked. "Not by the river in case it reminds you of the awful time when you were nearly drowned. Across the common and back through the wood."

Joanna cantered across the common and Twinkle did his comfortable, smooth, slow canter, easy for Joanna to sit down in the saddle and keep Gay steady. When Kim was there and went on in front Twinkle was apt to pull and to try and race him.

They went up a lane to the top of the hill and then turned into a gateway leading into the wood. The gate was missing, the ground was muddy and churned up and there were huge ruts full of water, for trees had been felled and dragged away by tractors. "Don't let's fall off here, Gay!" Joanna said, as Twinkle picked his way through the pools of muddy water.

They went down the track through the wood and Joanna wished she could see a squirrel, but she supposed they were all asleep now, and she pictured them curled up in holes in trees with their stores of nuts. The trees were bare and their branches were dark and lacy against the grey sky, it was a still day and the wood was very silent.

Almost frightening, Joanna thought, it was nice to have Twinkle and Gay for company, of course there was nothing to be frightened of in a wood. She was glad there were no wolves in England now, it would be very frightening to see them creeping towards you through the trees and to hear them howling. But there was nothing, no squirrels, not even a rabbit.

Thinking of rabbits made her wonder if Gay would like to run about in the wood, so she stopped and gently lowered Gay to the ground. She looked round and then started to sniff and ran on ahead, friskily and with her tail well up, so Joanna knew she was enjoying it.

The track went straight across the wood and came out at a gate into a field, it then rambled down to a farm, beyond which was a lane which would be a short way home. When they reached the end of the wood Joanna saw that the gateway was even wetter and muddier than the first one had been. She'd better have Gay up on her saddle or she'd get simply filthy. She looked round to see where Gay could do her mounting block act and saw that there was a bank with a hedge growing on it along one side of the wood. Joanna couldn't get on holding Gay, and if she put her up first Gay was liable to slide about on the slippery surface. The bank was full of old rabbit holes and rather brambly but it would have to do. She rode up to it and called Gay.

She knew at once what Joanna wanted, but she couldn't find a place where she could scramble up, then a bramble caught in her coat and Joanna had to get off to undo it. At last Gay found a place where she could wriggle through the brambles and she stood on the bank looking at Joanna as if she were smiling, and with her tongue hanging out. The bank sloped back leaving a big gap between the top of it and the saddle, a much bigger jump than the neat little skip across which Gay did at home, so Joanna tried to get Twinkle nearer, he was coming up close to it when he suddenly began to plunge about and to struggle.

"Whoa boy, whoa." Joanna soothed him and leaned forward to look down and see what was upsetting him. He was tugging and struggling with one of his hind legs, and she saw that it was caught in a bit of wire.

Joanna jumped off and held him, patting his neck and calming him; he mustn't struggle or he'd hurt himself. Sprain his leg, or even break it, you often heard of a horse breaking a leg. When he was standing quietly she examined the wire. It was a piece of old rabbit wire which, half buried in leaves now, must have been along the side of the wood once. It was broken and rusty and Twinkle's hoof had gone right through the big mesh, but when she lifted his foot to pull it off she found that a loop of wire had pulled tight in a noose when Twinkle struggled. It was drawn tightly round his fetlock and she couldn't move it. It would have to be cut off.

What *could* she do? If only Penny were here to go for help. The woodmen weren't working here and no one would come through the wood. She couldn't leave Twinkle alone in case he struggled. If he didn't injure himself by wrenching his leg the wire would cut him badly.

"You couldn't go and fetch help, Gay? You

would if you were a dog in a book! Home, Gay, go home." Joanna pointed, but Gay wagged her tail and stood still. She wasn't going home like a dog in a book. She sat down beside Twinkle, who put his head down and blew gently down his nostrils at her.

That decided Joanna. If Gay would stay and keep Twinkle company he'd probably stand quietly while she fetched someone. What a good thing they were such friends. She took off her coat and gave it to Gay to sit on, it would show Gay that Joanna was coming back. And Gay always sat on Joanna's clothes if she left them on the floor.

"*Wait*, Gay. Stay here. Wait." She hoped Gay would remember what she'd taught her, but she'd never left her in a strange place or for longer than four or five minutes.

It was with great misgivings that Joanna left her two precious animals alone in the wood. She went slowly at first, turning to say, "Wait, stay there, Gay," as long as they were in sight. Once she'd splashed through the gateway into the field she ran as fast as she could, down the track to the farm.

A dog on a chain barked as she pushed open a wicket gate and then hurried up the path to bang on the door. Was Twinkle struggling? If Gay went away and tried to go home and got on a main road——

The door was opened by a woman in a red cardigan, a flowery apron and gum boots. Breathlessly Joanna told her, "My pony's got caught in some wire in the wood. Is there anyone who could come and get it off for me, please? As soon as possible."

"They're busy milking now," the woman said doubtfully.

"It's terribly urgent," Joanna urged, "he may be hurt if we can't get it off."

The woman came out and went down the path and into the yard where she opened the cow-shed door and called someone. Joanna had a glimpse of a line of black and white cows and the milking machine's tubes. Suppose the man wouldn't come? She shivered without her coat. A man came to the door—what a funny noise the milking machine made—and the woman told him, "The little girl's pony's caught in some wire in the wood."

"Where would that be?"

Joanna told him and he said, "I'll be along in about ten minutes."

She thanked them both and then went back up the hill. As she went through the gateway, with the water oozing cold and wet into her shoes, she was almost afraid of what she was going to see. Would Gay still be there, and if not would she be lost again? Twinkle, would he have hurt himself?

There was Twinkle standing with his head down and resting his hind foot. Gay was sitting bolt upright on Joanna's coat, she was watching anxiously, and when she saw Joanna she laid her ears back and smiled in her own way.

"Good, good girl, Gay!" Joanna petted her. "Poor old Twink. It won't be long now."

But it seemed a long time. Dusk was falling and it was quiet, almost creepy, in the wood. Joanna tried not to think about it, at any rate there weren't wolves! And she wasn't alone, for she'd Gay and Twinkle. A light went on in one of the windows at the farm house and she thought, supposing the man's forgotten and is having his tea? It must be more than ten minutes. If she was very late getting home her mother and Penny would be worried.

Gay growled and Joanna saw a sheep dog coming over the brow of the hill. In another minute she saw a man walking up the track.

"There you be then. I got some wire clippers as'll soon get this off." He was quiet and gentle with Twinkle who stood still while he cut the wire.

"There, 'tis off. Lucky it weren't barbed wire or he'd be badly cut about. He's all right, may have wrenched hisself a bit, pulling at it like, but nothing much. Maybe it'll be sore for a day or so."

Joanna thanked him. "I won't ride him in case it hurts him. I'll lead him back."

"This your little dog? You didn't bring 'm down to the farm?"

"No. I left her here. She likes Twinkle, the pony, they're friends, so I thought he'd stand quietly if they were together. I've taught her to stay where I tell her, but I've never left her so long before."

"You're a dab at training, I can see. Why, my sheep dog wouldn't do any better nor that."

Joanna was very pleased at this, and very proud of Gay. "Another adventure," she told her mother and Penny, when she got home, where she and Penny examined Twinkle carefully and bathed his fetlock in warm water. "Gay does have exciting things happen to her."

"It's really us they happen to," said Penny.

CHAPTER ELEVEN

"HAPPY CHRISTMAS!"

"I THINK Gay's name ought to be Sweedle!" said Penny, after they had all been into the town to do their Christmas shopping. "Wherever we went people said, 'Oh, what a sweet little poodle!'"

"What a sweee-tle poodle!" chanted Joanna. She kissed the curls on the top of Gay's head. "You are a Sweee-dle! Only I wish she was really mine. It's awful to think somebody might come and take her away."

"Surely not now," Penny said. "We've had her almost three months. Couldn't we refuse to let her go, Mummie?"

"Hardly, if the real owner turned up," Mrs. Maitland answered. "But it's strange no one has claimed her, and that the police haven't heard of any lost poodle."

"We could charge such a lot for keeping her all this time that they'd refuse to pay and we'd refuse to let her go," Joanna suggested.

Mrs. Maitland laughed. "We weren't obliged to keep her. We could have handed her over to the police, who'd have sent her to a lost dogs' home."

"Doesn't she look well now?" Penny said. "She's grown a little and she's not so thin."

"I wish I knew nobody would ever come for her," Joanna said. "It's horrid not knowing for certain that she can stay always."

"I'd like to know she was really ours," Penny agreed.

But Gay had really become Joanna's dog though all the Maitlands were very fond of her.

"Did you do all your Christmas shopping?" asked Mrs. Maitland.

"Yes." Joanna arranged her parcels on the table. "Can you guess which is yours, Mummie? No, don't—in case you do! Penny, you're not to feel them."

"I've got all mine too," Penny said. "Not long to Christmas."

"No school, no homework, heaps of time to ride and to be with the animals," said Joanna. "I'm going to train Gay to do some new things, to find me when I hide and to fetch things."

"I hope the weather's decent so we can ride every day," Penny said.

"Do you know, Mummie," said Joanna, rearranging her parcels, "Penny and me are going to be Vets. We'll have a brass plate with our names, Miss P. and Miss J. Maitland, and all those letters after them."

"A splendid idea," said Mrs. Maitland, "any work which relieves pain is very worth while."

"I decided when Gay got better," said Penny. "It was so marvellous seeing her get strong again."

Joanna went to put her parcels away in her half of the wardrobe in the room which she shared with Penny. Gay followed her, sniffed at the parcels, watched her with bright eyes and then ran off with one of her slippers. Joanna chased her and they had a game with it. Gay was delighted to have Joanna at home all day. She followed her everywhere, and Mr. and Mrs. Maitland remarked how fond of each other the two were and how tragic it would be if they had to part.

Meanwhile odd things were happening. Postmen came more often and had to be barked at, parcels smelling very interesting came from grocer and butcher, a tree arrived and was taken into the sitting-room. Gay pattered round, sniffing, investigating—she was very inquisitive—and there was a bustle and excitement in the air which the dogs noticed. Carol singers came after dark and the dogs had to be shut up to prevent their barking drowning the singing!

One morning early Joanna crept downstairs and flashed her torch on Gay in her basket. "Happy Christmas, Gay!" she whispered, and picked up the little warm, white dog. Back to bed she went with Gay under her arm. Gay licked Joanna's nose, she thought it great fun.

Inside the girls' room Joanna switched on the light and Penny sat up, blinking.

"Happy Christmas, Penny! Let's open our stockings."

"Happy Christmas!" yawned Penny. "If you're going to have Gay I must have Peter Popples. Wait for me."

She pulled on her dressing-gown and went downstairs. Gay sat beside Joanna, watching her while she felt her stocking. There was a scuffling and bumping on the stairs and then the door opened and Penny came in with Peter.

"Sh! Don't make such a row, Pete!"

Peter wagged his tail and grinned, with his tongue lolling out, and then jumped up on Penny's bed, where he lay stretched out in great comfort.

"Make room, Pete, you can't have the whole

bed!" Penny got into bed and they started to open their stockings. The first present Joanna took out was a little box of sweets. She gave one to Gay. This, and the feeling of excitement, went to Gay's head. She sat on the pillow beside Joanna, her dark eyes shining, and sniffed at everything that Joanna took out of the stocking. Then she began to pull things out herself.

The most exciting things came out. Knives with tools for taking stones out of ponies' hooves, ties with horses' heads on them—Joanna had blue and Penny green—diaries, little china animals, pens that wrote three colours, little boxes of sweets and chocolates. Gay sniffed, licked or tasted everything. When the oranges in the toes of the stockings were reached the children knew that they had emptied their stockings. They got up and made tea to take to Mr. and Mrs. Maitland.

As soon as they opened the bedroom door, Scuttle, who slept at the foot of Mrs. Maitland's bed because she refused to sleep anywhere else, growled at Peter and Gay.

"Happy Christmas, Mummie. Happy Christmas, Daddy. We made you some tea." Penny put the tray on the little table and kissed her mother.

"Happy Christmas!" said Joanna, and climbed

under the eiderdown on her father's bed. "I can't come on your bed, Mummie, because Scoot would be so cross with Gay." Gay was under Joanna's arm. "We had smashing stockings!"

"Super stockings!" Penny said, tucking herself under her mother's eiderdown. "Shut up, Scoot, Peter's not coming on the bed."

Scuttle stopped growling and watched the tea tray. It had a sugar basin on it. She was hardly ever given sugar, but you never know your luck——

"May she, Mummie?" asked Penny. "It is Christmas Day, and Peter and Gay have had sweets in our room."

"Gay sat beside me on my pillow and helped me undo everything; once she'd had a sweet out of the first parcel to come out she was mad about taking presents out of stockings!" Joanna said.

"All right, it is Christmas Day!" Mrs. Maitland said. "But they'll all have to have one or Gay and Peter won't understand why they're left out."

The dogs crunched their sugar and thought what a day this was! It had certainly started well.

"I'm longing for the Tree and our presents," said Joanna.

"There's lots to do before then," Mrs. Maitland said. "I think it's time I got up."

"I think we must all help a great deal today," Mr. Maitland said. "Christmas is a very busy time for mums."

"We'll help," Penny said. "Let's get dressed, Jo."

The excitement continued. The sitting-room door was locked and the curtains were drawn. The most delicious smell spread through the house and the dogs spent the morning in the kitchen. Mrs. Maitland turned them out several times but they sneaked in again. That wonderful scent of something roasting drew them there.

After church Joanna took them for a run round the garden while Penny helped her mother. Lunch was very special, that smell made the dogs sit beside people's chairs and beg for tit-bits, a thing they were never allowed to do on ordinary days. "What a lot humans eat!" Scuttle said enviously. But at last lunch was over.

Penny had a piece of crisp, brown turkey skin for each of the dogs which she gave them after lunch. "Just because it's Christmas!" At last the washing up was done and the dining-room tidied. Joanna and Penny waited for the sitting-room door to be opened.

Mrs. Maitland flung it open. There, glittering in

the darkened room, was the Tree. Magic sight, lovelier than ever each year, Joanna thought. It stood in front of a long mirror which reflected the gleaming lights, the dark branches and the coloured presents hanging from them, so that it might have been two trees. After it had been admired Mr. Maitland switched on the light and the parcels heaped under the tree became visible.

"Ooh!" Joanna said, wondering which were for her.

"What a pretty tree!" said Mr. Maitland. "Let's admire it a little!"

"Oh, Daddy!" said Joanna, "do start giving the presents."

"It seems a pity to take things off it and spoil it!" teased her father.

"Do start, Daddy," Joanna said.

"Come on, Daddy!" urged Penny.

"Suppose we keep it. It would do for next year!"

"Do begin!" Joanna almost shrieked.

"Very well," Mr. Maitland sighed. "But it's a shame to spoil a lovely tree! What's this? A present for Stalky!"

Joanna undid it. A sugar mouse! "He'll love it," she said hopefully. But he didn't and Scuttle ate it.

Next Mr. Maitland handed two little parcels to Penny. One was labelled Penny from Jenny and the other Jenny from Penny. Jenny's was a large raisin. "Her favourite treat!" said Penny. Her tiny parcel contained the smallest china white rat ever seen for Penny's collection of china animals.

"I hope Gay gets something!" Joanna said.

"Mummie's turn," said Mr. Maitland and handed Mrs. Maitland a parcel; while she was undoing this Joanna had a parcel labelled Gay. It was a ball. She also had a blue collar, Scuttle had a red one and Peter a brown one. Jack had a string of very cheap shiny beads which he hid—jackdaws like doing this—and a tomato, one of his best-liked tit-bits.

Undoing presents took all the afternoon, and at last the Tree was bare and the pile of parcels was no more. The last things to be taken off the Tree were two large carrots, scrubbed and labelled Kim and Twinkle.

"Let's take these to the ponies before it's quite dark," said Joanna.

"A run in the garden will do the dogs good," Penny agreed. "They've been indoors most of the day."

"Tea will be ready when you come in," said

Mrs. Maitland, who was doing that most boring job, picking up paper and string and tidying the room.

"It was a lovely Tree," said Joanna, "and every one of the animals had something. Thank you, Mummie."

"Yes, I thought it would be fun to put something on it for each of them, but of course they can't understand. Their thoughts and feelings are different from people's."

"But I'm glad they weren't left out," Penny said.

"Always remember that people are more important than animals though," said Mrs. Maitland.

"Isn't Christmas super!" Joanna said, as Twinkle crunched his carrot. "And isn't it sad to think it's a whole year before it comes again!"

"An awful long time," Penny agreed. "Mummie's been frightfully busy. Let's do everything tonight and not let her do a thing."

Joanna thought this a good idea. They gave hay to the ponies, fed Jack, and coaxed Stalky indoors.

Tea was ready. The table was lit by big red candles; cake, crackers—everything looked Christmassy and cosy.

"No more work for you today, Mummie," said

Penny. "Joanna and I are going to do everything. You sit still."

"Thank you, darling, that will be lovely," she said.

Penny thought, after they had cleared away tea, prepared supper and washed up, that there was a very satisfactory feeling about doing the work and knowing that their mother was having a rest.

"The best Christmas we've ever had," she said. But she didn't know what tomorrow held in store for them.

CHAPTER TWELVE

THE SCOOT POOT DID IT!

IT was a fine morning on Boxing Day and, as they dressed, Penny and Joanna planned to go for a long ride. They went out before breakfast to feed the animals and took two hay-nets to the ponies.

As soon as they reached the paddock they knew something was wrong. Twinkle was trotting about and neighing and there was no sign of Kim.

"Bother him!" exclaimed Penny. "He's got out, he would do it today."

Joanna tied up a hay-net and Twinkle, who was glad to see them, snatched a mouthful of hay and then walked away, looking all round.

"He's always restless if he's alone," Joanna said. "He hates being away from Kim but he isn't clever enough to go too, luckily!"

"We'll have to search for Kim after breakfast," said Penny. "He doesn't usually go far."

"I'll ride Twinkle," said Joanna. "He'll have digested his hay by the time we're ready to start."

"Someone may see Kim and ring us up to tell us," said Penny. "Everyone round here knows him."

After breakfast they set out. Joanna riding Twinkle went one way and Penny, on her bike, went the other. They asked everyone they met if they'd seen a pony. It wasn't the first time Kim had got out, and they always conducted their search in this way. Joanna trotted along keeping to by-roads. There were few people about since it was Boxing Day, no postmen, bakers' vans or roadmen, but after she had gone several miles she came to a small village and asked some boys if anyone had seen a pony. Since they were sure no one had, Joanna turned back and hoped that Penny had met with better luck.

She was quite near her home when an overtaking car pulled up beside her and the driver leaned out calling to her, "Have you lost a pony by any chance?"

"Yes. A dark brown Exmoor."

"I know where he is," the lady driving the car said, "he's quite safe. He was caught on the road and shut in at a farm at Welford. I've just come from there. The people's name is West." She gave Joanna their telephone number.

"Thank you awfully." Joanna trotted home to find Penny had just returned from a long and fruitless ride.

"Welford. That's quite a a long way," Penny said.

"Ring up and say we'll fetch him this afternoon," said Mrs. Maitland. "I'll take you over in the car directly after lunch."

Mrs. Maitland took Penny, with Kim's saddle and bridle, and Joanna and Gay, Scuttle and Peter Popples, and drove to Welford. When they arrived at the Wests' house a boy and a girl were at the gate looking out for them.

"I believe you've got our pony?" asked Mrs. Maitland.

"Yes," replied the boy, "we caught him and put him in a stable at the farm opposite. The farmer said we'd better, in case he got knocked down by a car."

"It was very good of you," said Mrs. Maitland.

"Thanks awfully," Penny said. "He's never gone far when he's got out before."

"We must have the fence made more secure," said Mrs. Maitland.

The boy and girl, who said their names were Richard and Jennifer, took them to the farm where

Kim, shut in a stable, seemed pleased to see them and to come out of the stable. He and Penny set off for home at a spanking trot.

"Three dogs!" Jennifer said, looking at the car. "And ponies, you are lucky!"

"And a cat, a jackdaw and a white rat!" Joanna said.

"How smashing!" said Richard. "What are the dogs called?"

"Peter, Scuttle and Gay."

"We knew someone who had a poodle called Gay, but last summer she got lost," Jennifer said.

There was a moment's silence, and Joanna felt sick.

Mrs. Maitland asked quietly, "Where was it lost and when?"

"It was at the end of the summer hols, just before we went back to school," said Jennifer. "We went for a picnic on the downs with the Masons, and Gay ran off."

"It must be her," said Mrs. Maitland in a shaky voice. Glancing at Joanna, she thought she looked quite stunned. "Get in the car, darling," she said. Turning to Richard she asked for the Masons' address, and then said good-bye and drove off.

"It must be her," Joanna said miserably. "It

wasn't far from the downs where we found her, and it was just the time they lost theirs. We started school directly after that."

"I'm afraid so," said Mrs. Maitland. "I'm so very sorry."

"If Kim hadn't got out and come here we'd not have found out," said Joanna.

"We should have sooner or later, I expect."

"What are you going to do, Mummie?"

"I must ring the Masons up and tell them."

Joanna sat in silence, hugging Gay, all the way home. The thing she had dreaded had happened. Gay was going to be taken from her.

"Poor Joanna," thought Mrs. Maitland. "After such a happy Christmas, and she enjoyed it so with Gay; and poor little dog, she's so fond of us that she'll hate going, even if she is going back to her original owners. Poor Joanna will be dreadfully sad."

When they overtook Penny they stopped to tell her.

"Gosh! How sickening!" said Penny. "How rotten, Jo."

Joanna didn't answer. She bent her head over Gay—she couldn't talk about it yet.

Mrs. Maitland rang up Mrs. Mason as soon as

they got home. She wanted to get it over. It was certainly Gay. The Masons had lost her two days before Penny and Joanna had found her. They would certainly want her back. Barbara had been upset at losing her.

"My little girl has become very fond of Gay," Mrs. Maitland said. "In fact we all have. Gay was very ill when she first came here and we nursed her through it and now she's so fond of us that I think it will distress her to leave us. And Joanna, my girl, will be heart-broken. Would you sell her to us?"

"No," Mrs. Mason thought not. "Barbara had been given the poodle and had wanted one so much. They are nervy little things, aren't they? Easily scared. Gay just ran away on the downs, we thought something frightened her but we couldn't think what it was. We'll come over and get her tomorrow."

"Could you come in the morning?" asked Mrs. Maitland. She knew Joanna was going to be very unhappy at Gay leaving them and she thought it would be best to get it over quickly.

When she told them that the Masons were coming to fetch Gay, Joanna burst into tears.

"I know how much you mind," said Mrs. Maitland, "but we can't do anything about it. I tried to buy Gay from them but they wouldn't sell her."

"Couldn't we get another puppy for Joanna?" Penny whispered to her mother. "A poodle puppy like Gay? I could help pay for it with my Christmas present money."

"That's a very nice idea. I'll ask Daddy what he thinks. It wouldn't make up for losing Gay but it would help Joanna to get over it."

Everyone spent a sad evening. Gay was particularly affectionate to Joanna. She knew something was going to happen, something affecting her, and it made her anxious, so she kept close to Joanna and followed her everywhere.

The next morning Joanna took Gay into the garden. She dawdled about, letting Jack out, going to see the ponies, throwing Gay's ball, she couldn't settle to anything. She dreaded hearing the Masons' car arrive to take Gay away, but she would be glad when it was over.

To part with Gay—Gay with her pretty little face and bright, dark eyes, the little curls on top of her head, the way she played and tore round the lawn or sat at Joanna's feet with her forepaws crossed, the dainty way she danced on her hind legs—Joanna gulped when she thought of losing her.

It was marvellous of Mummie to say that she and Penny would get her a puppy for her own, but Joanna knew she'd given a little bit of her heart to Gay that nothing could replace. And what about Gay, Joanna wondered? Would she be happy with the Masons? She'd run away, so perhaps they weren't nice to her. Joanna shuddered at the thought of Gay being unhappy. Gay, lively and high-spirited, full of mischief, supposing she became dejected and miserable—if only the Masons would sell her to them!

She heard the car and went indoors with Gay to find Mrs. Mason, smiling and jolly, and Barbara, who looked discontented and peevish.

"That's Gay," Mrs. Mason declared. "She's grown a bit, hasn't she, Barbara? Come, Gay! Gay!" Mrs. Mason snapped her fingers and Gay went slowly up to her. Then she put her tail down and went back to Joanna.

"She's very fond of Joanna," said Mrs. Maitland.

"She'll soon get used to us again," said Mrs. Mason with a laugh. "See if she remembers you, Barbara, she should do."

Barbara called Gay, and when Gay didn't go to her she went across to her and stroked her. Gay sniffed Barbara's hand and then retreated behind Joanna. She had had no love or understanding from Barbara, and though she couldn't understand that Barbara had come to take her away, she remembered the unhappy days she had spent at the Masons'. She sat beside Joanna, quivering and anxious.

"She doesn't know me," Barbara said. "She's silly."

"She's got fond of us now," explained Joanna.

"She was very ill when we found her," said Penny, "and we looked after her and nursed her so she got to depend on us. And of course we all love her." Penny disliked the Masons, she thought they weren't fond of Gay.

"I wish you'd let us buy her," said Mrs. Maitland. "Or we could get you another poodle puppy, if you like."

"We'd rather have Gay," replied Mrs. Mason. "I don't like small puppies, they're too much trouble. I let Barbara have Gay because she was older and trained."

"What's that one called?" Barbara asked, pointing to Scuttle who, as usual, was sitting on Mrs. Maitland's lap.

"Scuttle."

"Why do you call her that?"

"Because when she was a small puppy she used to gallop round the kitchen very fast," explained Mrs. Maitland, "and we used to say she was scuttling about."

Barbara went across and stooped to pat her. Scuttle, defensive of Mrs. Maitland, her beloved mistress, sprang up growling and snapped at Barbara, who gave a loud yell.

"Scuttle!" Mrs. Maitland exclaimed, and gave her a slap. "I am sorry, Barbara, she's never snapped at anyone before. She didn't hurt you, I hope?"

Mrs. Mason was fussing over Barbara and inspecting her face. "She isn't hurt but she might have been bitten, scarred perhaps. What a dangerous dog!"

"I really am sorry," apologized Mrs. Maitland. "I've never known her snap at people, though she won't let other dogs come near me if she's on my lap. I'm so glad she didn't hurt you, Barbara."

Barbara snivelled; she'd had a scare. "I don't like snappy dogs."

"I didn't know poodles were snappy or I wouldn't have had one," Mrs. Mason said.

Mrs. Maitland was about to say she'd never

known a snappy poodle when she changed her mind and said nothing.

Penny was speaking. "Oh, I've heard of poodles that bite and snap. Any dog will at times. And poodles are such good guards, you see, and so excitable. Gay's a very good guard already."

Mrs. Mason looked doubtful. "I hope Gay won't get snappy."

Penny went on, "She easily might. She snaps at Scuttle over bones, and if Joanna leaves any of her clothes about Gay sits on them and won't let anyone touch them."

"Oh dear!" Mrs. Mason said. "I don't know what to say. I don't want a snappy dog."

"Why don't you have a cocker spaniel?" suggested Penny. "Like Peter. They're awfully good-tempered and friendly." She was feeling excited, there was a chance that it would work. These were horrid people, not a bit fond of Gay, and if they took her both Gay and Joanna would be miserable. Why, they'd never shown any pleasure at getting Gay back. They didn't deserve a dog. Penny attacked again.

"Of course even spaniels can get snappy. If I were you I'd have a Siamese cat. They're absolutely wizard and just as intelligent as dogs." A cat looks after itself better than a puppy does, thought Penny; it wouldn't be so miserable if it wasn't made a real pet of as a puppy would.

"A Siamese cat!" Mrs. Mason repeated. "They're very pretty but it's not quite the same as having a dog. What do you think, Barbara darling?"

"Cats scratch," said Barbara sulkily.

"Not Siamese," said Penny. "Not if you treat 'em well." And if you don't, she thought, it serves you right!

Peter walked across to Mrs. Maitland and Scuttle growled.

"There, you see," said Penny. "You never know if they'll snap."

"What do you think, Mrs. Maitland, would Gay get snappy?" asked Mrs. Mason.

"I wouldn't like to say," answered Mrs. Maitland truthfully.

"I don't think I'll risk having a dog, in case Barbara got bitten. Would you like a cat, Barbara?"

"Yes. A Siamese, or a blue Persian."

"Then we'll leave Gay with you," said Mrs. Mason.

Joanna, who had been listening with unbearable anxiety, felt too happy for belief. "Gay! Oh, how marvellous!" She hugged Gay, who licked her face.

"Will you let me pay you for her?" asked Mrs. Maitland.

Mrs. Mason hesitated. "Well, you've kept her all this time and she does seem to have settled down here. Let Joanna have her for her own."

"Oh, thank you!" cried Joanna.

"I'd like to pay for her so we feel she's really ours, please," Mrs. Maitland insisted. She didn't want to risk them changing their minds and saying Barbara wanted Gay back. A price was decided upon and Mrs. Maitland wrote a cheque for Mrs. Mason, and then they drove away.

"Look at those two dashing round the lawn," said Mrs. Maitland. "They're both mad with joy!"

Gay and Joanna were going full tilt. Joanna felt she would burst with happiness, and Gay was racing with her. The big black cloud that Gay had felt hanging over them was gone. Joanna was happy so Gay was too, she yapped shrilly.

Penny squeezed her mother's arm. "Wasn't it smashing! Good old Scoot Poot! She did it and I rubbed it in!"

"You did exaggerate, darling!"

"I know. They weren't fond of Gay, they never

petted her or seemed pleased to have found her. I hope they don't have another dog, a cat would stick up for itself better. Gay didn't like them. And they never thanked us for keeping her and getting her well again."

"No, they took it for granted," agreed Mrs. Maitland. "Thank goodness it's turned out like this."

Joanna and Gay came tearing up to them. Joanna flung her arms round her mother.

"Oh, Mummie! It's wonderful. Thank you for buying her, it's the best Christmas present I ever had. Gay's really mine now."

"Yes, it gave us a bad fright, thinking they would take her away but now it's settled for good," answered Mrs. Maitland.

"I must go and see Twinkle and Kim and show them that Gay's still here. They probably guessed that something was wrong, they're such friends—Gay and the ponies." And Joanna raced off with Gay close at her heels.